AN AVALON HISTORICAL ROMANCE

CHANCES
A Love's Valley Romance

Carolyn Brown

Adelida Broussau took a big chance by saying she was Rueben Hamilton's new bride. Her sister, Maria, was dead. Her brother-in-law, Victor, ordered her out of New Orleans by nightfall. Then there was Rueben, hit on the head for attempting to thwart a bank robbery, his memory gone and leaving town that very day. So she took a big chance and let him believe they were married.

Rueben Hamilton went to New Orleans at the request of the President to help with the reconstruction of Louisiana after the Civil War. He'd gone into the bank to finish his business before boarding *The Queen* for the first leg of his journey home. He didn't remember the bank robbery. All he remembered was awaking with a headache, no memory, and a wife.

It was supposed to take a month for them to reach Love's Valley, Pennsylvania. That was if everything went according to plan and Rueben's memory didn't return. But fate played her hand and dealt the two of them some unforeseen cards that turned their world upside down.

Their hearts didn't care that there'd been a war and it was the worst possible time for a Yankee soldier and a Louisiana bayou woman to fall in love.

CHANCES

A Love's Valley Historical Romance

•

Carolyn Brown

AVALON BOOKS

NEW YORK

Published by Thomas Bouregy & Co., Inc.
160 Madison Avenue, New York, NY 10016

Library of Congress Cataloging-in-Publication Data

Brown, Carolyn, 1948–
    Chances / Carolyn Brown.
        p. cm.
    ISBN 0-8034-9756-3 (alk. paper)
    1. Bank robberies—Fiction. 2. Amnesia—Fiction.
3. New Orleans (La.)—Fiction. 4. Louisiana—Fiction.
5. Pennsylvania—Fiction. 6. Domestic fiction. I. Title.

PS3552.R685275C43 2006
813'.54—dc22

                                        2005028546

PRINTED IN THE UNITED STATES OF AMERICA
ON ACID-FREE PAPER
BY HADDON CRAFTSMEN, BLOOMSBURG
PENNSYLVANIA

To Dennis and Donna Brown

Chapter One

Adelida Broussau's stomping on the wooden sidewalk sounded like a herd of full-grown stampeding elephants, but the outward noise was nothing compared to the beating of a very angry heart deep inside her breast. *Victor LaSalle should be shot and fed to the 'gaters,* she thought to herself. *No, forget the waste of a good bullet. Just throw him, warm and alive, to the 'gaters. He was nothing but a spy for the Yankees and no self-respecting Louisiana man would consort with those low-down Yankees.*

But then no one had ever accused Victor of having a healthy dose of self respect. What Victor had was a triple dose of pure greed. Sitting in his big house, eating crawfish and rice from a silver spoon. He'd made a fortune spying on his own people. Adelida knew all about it and had begun to think the bullet that took her sister's life had been meant for her.

How could a Louisiana-born Cajun go against his roots and his upbringing like Victor had done? It was a mystery to Adelida. But she didn't have time to dwell on her brother-in-law's faults and failures. Not when there

wasn't one single penny left in her reticule and probably
very little money left in the account Maria had set up in
the Louisiana State Bank just down the street. Why had
she let her sister talk her into spending so much money on
pretty frocks?

"Because you didn't expect your sister to die, or for
Victor to put you out of the house the minute he heard his
wife was dead and say he would kill you if you weren't out
of New Orleans before sundown tonight," she muttered.

Mercy, but it was sweltering hot even at ten o'clock in
the morning. Everything drooped in the sticky humidity
where a breeze couldn't be begged, borrowed, bought or
stolen. Flags hung limp. Of course, there were no more
Rebel flags, and if one happened to be discovered, it
would be right next door to treason. Or sin. According to
the new order of things, a Rebel flag found in the possession of a ninety-year-old nun would put her in prison
and keep her out of heaven for sure. Spring flowers hung
their heads in total shame. Nothing had a bit of energy
except Adelida Broussau.

Henry Rueben Hamilton swatted a mosquito the size of
a healthy, well-fed Love's Valley buzzard from his cheek,
then held his aching head for a moment before he crossed
the street to the Louisiana State Bank. He squinted against
the harsh, unforgiving sun.

What had Lewis been thinking by marrying that girl on
the spur of the moment? Lewis and he had dragged the
poor preacher out of bed after midnight to do the ceremony in the moonlit courtyard of a friend, and Rueben
had then spent the rest of the night toasting the newly
wedded couple over and over again. He hadn't even gotten an hour's sleep.

He and Lewis were supposed to be boarding the steamship to Baltimore taking them on the first leg of the journey home that morning. From there, they would have traveled on by stage or train to central Pennsylvania. But Rueben would have to go it alone now that his best friend and second cousin had decided to stay on in Louisiana and work for his new wife's father in the shipping business. At least Rueben would have the whole room to himself and he wouldn't have to listen to Lewis snoring in the next bed. He'd have days and days to catch up on nights of missed sleep. Once his business at the bank was finished, he planned to crawl into the bed in his private stateroom on the fancy steamship and sleep for the whole day and night. He might not wake up for the whole two-and-a-half weeks up the coast to Baltimore, Maryland.

Without Lewis to keep him company it was sure to be another long, dull trip anyway. Days and days of nothing but water and short visits to shore when they stopped at various ports of call. He remembered a similar trip more than a year ago when he came to Louisiana. Lewis had already been sent, so he'd been on his own, and the days had been long, hot, and utterly boring.

Dreading the trip back to Love's Valley, near Shirleysburg, Pennsylvania, he wished he was already there with his family. He was so consumed with his self-pity that he wasn't watching at all where he was going.

Adelida came from the opposite direction, her head down as she berated Victor and mourned the death of her sister. She wished she'd never left the bayou, sold her father's *bateau* or went to that play. She also was not watching where she was going.

The two of them met, quite literally, in a collision that sent them to the ground—a tumble of petticoats, lace-edged drawers, flailing legs and arms.

Adelida thought she'd run into a brick wall and half of

it had come tumbling down on top of her. She opened her eyes, gasping to regain the breath that had been violently knocked from her lungs. There were no bricks, but a handsome man pinned her down to the sidewalk. Rueben attempted to roll off the lovely lady, but got his boots tangled up in her skirt tails and landed on top of her again.

"So sorry. Pardon me for not watching where I was going, madame," he stuttered and stammered, finally finding a toehold that didn't involve battling the lady's undergarments. Red-faced, he offered her a hand, which she pushed away with a powerful flick of her tiny wrist and stood up on her own power.

"It is enough," she glared at him.

"I agree," he nodded. "It is enough. Again, I am so very sorry. I was deep in my own thoughts and wasn't watching where I was going. Are you all right, madame? Are you harmed in any way? Could I escort you into the bank?"

She brushed dust from her skirt and fixed her hat at a right angle, retying the satin bow off to one side with a flourish. "I am fine and yes, you may escort me into the bank," she said.

He offered his arm, confused as to what a woman was doing outside with no proper chaperone or escort.

"Thank you," she took his arm. She'd never dealt with bankers without her sister, Maria, beside her. Perhaps they would pay more attention to a woman on the arm of a gentleman.

"Please allow me to introduce myself. I am Henry Rueben Hamilton. Most people call me Rueben," he said, as he opened the door and allowed her to enter the huge, two-story building on Royal Street.

"And I am Adelida Broussau," she said.

Rueben liked the softness of her southern accent. The mosquitoes, he could do without; the sweltering heat, he'd gladly leave behind; but the sweet, soft accents of the women, now that was something he would miss when he got home to Pennsylvania. Adelida's voice sounded like someone had mixed the finest Kentucky bourbon with pure Love's Valley honey. Just enough sweetness to offset the huskiness, the end result melting a man's defenses into a heap of raw desire. Of course, he told himself, he'd never take one of these southern women home with him. Lewis was crazy to marry a southerner so soon after the war. Even if his wife's family accepted him, there would be those who didn't, and it wouldn't be easy living in the South when he'd fought on the Union side of the war. When the time came, Rueben would marry his own kind, most likely someone from right near Love's Valley. And that was a fact that could be chiseled into stone and set at the base of the altar in his church in central Pennsylvania. But he wouldn't think about that today, not even with a pretty woman on his arm.

"It is surely going to be a hot day, but it's my last one in Louisiana. I'm leaving this muggy place and going home," he said, talking more than he normally did to strangers, but still embarrassed about landing on top of her right there on the sidewalk.

"Oh?" She didn't care where he came from or what he was doing in Louisiana, but she did need to keep him engaged in conversation until she withdrew the pitiful little amount left in her account.

"Yes, my ship, *The Queen*, leaves this morning to take me to Baltimore, Maryland. From there I'll go on home by train and coach," he explained. "Well, here we are. You may have this one. I'll take the one on the far end." He nodded toward another teller without a line in front of his window.

"Thank you," she said.

"And again, I do apologize for the incident out there. You have a good day, Adelida," he smiled.

"You as well, and have a safe journey home," she told him.

"Could I help you, ma'am?" the man behind the window asked.

"I would like to withdraw all the funds from my account. Adelida Broussau. It was set up in both my name and my sister's. Maria LaSalle."

"I'm terribly sorry, Miss Broussau," the teller flipped through a book on his desk. "That account was closed yesterday afternoon. Of course, you do realize that anything with Mrs. LaSalle's name instantly became the property of her husband as soon as she died. Mr. Victor LaSalle took all the money from the account and closed it."

"That swamp rat," she hissed. The room did a couple of quick spins before she got things under control. Victor had won again. What on earth was she going to do?

Rueben stepped up to the window and commenced his own business, noting that Adelida had taken a seat on a bench in the middle of the lobby. Whatever the teller had said, had washed all the color from her face. It wasn't Rueben's nature to pry, even if he and the lady had fallen into each other's arms, but he did wonder what had happened.

He'd barely had time to pocket the money the teller had meticulously counted out to him when a loud booming voice behind him announced that everyone was to stay calm. He turned quickly to see three men brandishing shot guns, the lower half of their faces covered with bandannas. Rueben rolled his eyes toward the high ceiling. Wasn't that just his luck? The bank was being robbed and they'd probably take his money as well.

"You, get over there with the little woman waiting on

you," the biggest of the three men pointed the gun at his chest and nodded toward Adelida.

"She's not waiting on me," Rueben said, moving toward the center of the room, the man right behind him.

"Sure, she's not," the man chuckled. "We been in this bank for half an hour waiting for the right minute to do this job. We saw you come in with her, mister, so don't try to protect her."

"I'm not waiting on anyone," Adelida said. "I don't even know this man."

"Don't try to protect him neither, woman," the man said. "This is a robbery. So you people back there behind them windows, fill up the bags my friends are giving you."

Rueben eased his hand into his coat toward the gun he carried in a shoulder holster. If he could get to his pistol, he might be able to stop the robbery or at least put a kink in their plans if he threatened to kill the big man closest to him. His fingers were wrapping around the butt of the pistol when he noticed a movement in his peripheral vision. Instantly, everything in the room went black and he was falling through space into a deep, dark hole.

"What have you done?" Adelida tried to catch Rueben as he fell, but only fell down hard on the floor with the man's bleeding head in her lap.

"I kept your husband from shooting me," the robber told her bluntly. "He tried to be a hero, and I cold-cocked him one for it. You're just lucky I didn't shoot him."

Adelida didn't even try to explain again that Rueben Hamilton was not her husband. It made no difference to these wicked men. Blood ran freely from the cut on Rueben's head, soaking through her skirt.

The man who'd waited on Adelida filled the bag with money and then deftly reached under the counter for his own weapon, a Colt pistol with six rounds. He could shoot the man in front of him and perhaps the other two in the melee that would follow. A grin split his thin face as visions of heroism clouded his common sense. Before he raised the gun two inches from its hiding place, one of the robbers shot him from less than three feet away with a shotgun. The teller was dead before he hit the floor.

Adelida's screams could be heard above both of the other women in the bank.

"Shut your mouth or your husband will have more than a little bump on the head," the man said, pointing the gun at Rueben's chest. "Get those bags filled or there'll be more than one dead man in this bank," he shouted above the sobs of the other women.

Adelida hushed, but her heart pounded in her chest. She didn't even know the man bleeding in her lap, but she didn't want him to die because she couldn't stop screaming. She dropped her eyes to stare at Rueben. Dark hair and heavy lashes fanned out on his handsome face. Dark brows. A fine-looking man who did not deserve to die.

"Let's go. There's people looking in the window. Must've heard the shot," the man in charge yelled. The three men ran out the front door and jumped onto waiting horses. A cloud of dust was all that was left by the time the bank president came running from a side office, screaming orders about the sheriff, the doctor, the money. Adelida was too terrified to stand, too numb with the shock to do anything but sit there with a strange man's head in her lap.

"I'm so very sorry," the man wrung his hands as people scattered to do his bidding.

Adelida wondered why he was apologizing to her. It was the handsome young man with his head in her lap who should be receiving apologies. She sat there, mute in fear and numb in the knowledge that she had no place to go when she stood up.

The doctor arrived in what seemed like a blink of the eye to Adelida. She heard him tell them the man in the teller cage was dead. Then he was beside her, checking Rueben's pulse and opening the top of a well-worn black bag. "Got him pretty good, but head wounds look worse than they are. At least he's alive. Someone get me some water in a basin and let's get this young man cleaned up."

Adelida watched in silence as he washed away the blood and stitched the wound that the butt of the gun had created in Rueben's forehead. Then the doctor dressed the wound, wrapping white bandages snugly around his head. Just as he finished, Rueben's eyes opened.

"You are a lucky man," the doctor snapped his case shut. "Could have been much worse than it is and you didn't wake up until the stitching was done. Young lady, you take those out in ten days. They'll be itching by then. Why did you get a hit on the head when the teller was shot dead?"

"I think he was reaching for a gun and the robber hit him with the shotgun," Adelida said.

"Who are you? What's going on? Where am I?" Rueben said, a blank look in his eyes. He couldn't remember one thing.

"Looks like you got a concussion, too," the doctor said. "It'll pass in a while. Might take a few days or even a few weeks, but one day you'll wake up and it will all come back to you. Works that way. Saw it in the war lots of times."

"Who am I?" Rueben asked, his brow furrowing in painful wrinkles as he tried to get a firm grip on something—his name, where he was.

"You are Henry Rueben Hamilton and you are going to Baltimore, Maryland, today on a ship called *The Queen*," Adelida said softly. Perhaps if she reminded him of that much, the rest would fall into place.

"See there," the doctor said. "Thank goodness this little woman knows you and can take care of you."

"Who are you?" Rueben looked up into the most beautiful face he'd ever seen. Maybe he was in heaven. She looked like a dark-haired angel.

Adelida had nothing left, not even enough money to hire a buggy back to the hotel where she had to check out by noon. She inhaled deeply and looked right down into the eyes of the man whose blood had stained her skirt, and then took the biggest chance she'd ever taken. "Don't you remember? I'm your new bride. We were married yesterday. I'm Mrs. Rueben Hamilton and we're going home on The *Queen* where you have passage booked for us. Remember?"

"No, I do not remember anything," Rueben said. "But I'm glad you do."

"That ship leaves this morning, I do believe," the doctor said. "Now, don't you worry, Mrs. Hamilton. His memory will come back. It might come in small doses or he might wake up one day and presto, there it will be. One never knows about the brain; it works its own magic. Complete rest and recuperation are what he needs after a blow like that to his head. Do you understand, ma'am, what I mean by complete rest?"

"Yes, sir," she said. "You can't tell me when he might remember?"

"No idea," the doctor said, giving her a hand getting Rueben outside to a taxi. "Could be parts of his memory will return in a few days. You can expect everything or nothing. Most of the time I've seen the long-term memory return first then the short-term, those two or three days around the actual day he was hurt take a bit longer."

"Thank you," she said, hoping that his short-term memory stayed buried long enough to get her far away from Victor LaSalle and his wicked temper.

"Take me to the Rue de Bateau, the hotel with the boat on the side," she told the taxi driver. "I'll need my trunk. Then please take us to *The Queen*."

The driver flicked the reins against two fine horses. "That ship leaves in only a little while."

"Then hurry," Adelida said. "Rueben, I'll need money to pay this man."

"What is the Rue de Bateau?" Rueben handed her his wallet and then groaned and laid his aching head back. Everything was a fog. He could remember being at a wedding and someone toasting the bride and groom, but he couldn't recollect saying vows. He must have married her, though. Why else would she be beside him, taking care of him?

"A hotel where we stayed last night. It's not far from the dock where The *Queen* is waiting," she said.

"Did I really get married?" he asked, without opening his eyes.

"You did," she said. "Did you hear the doctor giving me instructions for taking care of you? He said to take the stitches out in ten days and that we are to sleep in separate beds until your memory returns. It could be harmful to your brain to sleep with me," she blushed.

"Okay," he murmured. "Whatever you say."

His flat voice let Adelida know he wasn't from Louisiana, but she didn't care. She'd taken a tremendous chance. She'd sowed her seeds when she said she was this man's wife. It would definitely reap her a way out of Victor LaSalle's grasp, but the harvest might be a bleak one when his memory came back.

She'd face that later. Right then she had a ship to reach within the hour and a new husband in so much pain and bewilderment that he didn't care that she wasn't going to be sleeping with him.

Chapter Two

Rueben's head had a whole band marching through it, the drums pounding in his ears with every step. If only he could shake it vigorously, the pain would disappear and his memory would return. It was the strangest sensation to have a life as a grown man that was less than two hours long. How old was he? What was he doing in Louisiana? Did he have a family somewhere waiting for him? Questions and more questions fluttered around in the dense fog with no answers.

Adelida scanned the ship's room and the rich mahogany furnishings, polished to a gleaming shine. Thank goodness there were two beds instead of one. The room was a miniature slice of the magnificent villa where her sister had lived with Victor LaSalle. It was beyond her imagination that there could be mansions that floated on water. All she could hope for was that this big old bear of a man would stay in his amnesiac trance long enough that she could enjoy the room a few days before he kicked her off at some port.

"Did I really marry you? I remember a wedding but I

don't remember saying the words," Rueben said from the bed where the driver had laid him before returning for their trunks.

"Just rest. It will come back to you in good time. Forcing your sick brain to try to remember will only make it worse," she said. "Why don't you sleep while I unpack. Maybe when you awake you will know everything."

But I hope not. Not just yet, she thought. *Please, I will wait on you hand and foot if I can just get away from New Orleans and that wicked Victor. I've always despised that man, but I never realized how much he disliked me before now. I must remind him that he was just a bayou fisherman. He probably doesn't want me around in case I poke holes in the fake past he's created for himself.*

Rueben shut his eyes and tried desperately to remember something—anything. Their trunks were brought in. Adelida opened his wallet and paid the man. Then she busied herself unpacking a huge trunk. He tried to sleep, but the pain was so bad he couldn't. He opened his eyes and watched her. Surely, he would recollect marrying such a beauty. There was a wedding. He was sure of that. He could remember a bride in a white lace veil. He drew his brow down in a serious frown, trying to remember the rest of the ceremony. The only thing that came to mind were champagne glasses and toasting the newlyweds.

"Tell me again what happened," he rolled over on one side, drew his knees up, and wrapped his arms around the extra pillow.

His voice startled Adelida. She'd thought for sure he was sound asleep and wouldn't wake for hours. She took a deep breath and kept working. "We were in the bank for you to finish your business in New Orleans," she said. That part was easy since it was the truth. "There was a robbery and you thought you could stop the men. Only the man in charge hit you on the head with the butt of his shotgun. After the men rode off with the money, the doctor came and stitched your forehead. Don't worry, it won't scar your pretty face too much. You didn't remember anything when you came to, not even me."

"Did we know each other very long before we married?" he asked. Maybe if she recounted the romance, it would come back to him in a flash.

"Not long. Three weeks. You insisted at the last moment that we get married and that I go home with you," she said, deliberately keeping her voice calm and collected, even though her palms were clammy.

A knock on the door made both of them jump. Rueben sat straight up in the bed and held his throbbing head with one hand. Adelida made her weak knees carry her to the door. Who would she find behind the door? Was a real wife joining him? A family member or a friend who would know she was an impostor? Her clammy hands slipped on the gold-plated knob, and there was a second knock before she could twist it enough to open the door.

"Who are you?" The blond-haired, blue-eyed man had been smiling, but it faded so fast his muscles scarcely had time to readjust themselves.

"Who are *you*?" she stammered only slightly.

"Rueben?" The man waltzed right into the room without an invitation. "What is going on here?"

"Who are you?" Rueben asked. "Do I know you from somewhere? Are you by any chance related to me?"

"Is this some kind of joke?" the man asked.

"I'm afraid not," Rueben said. "But if I know you, it would be a great help if you'd tell me who you are and any information about myself. I can't remember a thing."

"Rueben tried to stop a bank robbery today," Adelida explained. "For his efforts he got hit in the forehead with the butt of a gun. The doctor says it might be a while before his memory comes back. Who are you? Are you family?"

"I'm Rueben's friend, John Jacobs. I've been stationed with him for the past six months. I'm on my way home to Florida. He and his cousin, Lewis, had this room booked for the journey to Baltimore," he said.

"So I was in the army?" Rueben asked. "Tell me more."

"You were sent down here by the President himself to help with the reconstruction of Louisiana after the war. You and Lewis were going home today. He's supposed to be in this room with you, not some Cajun woman," he narrowed his eyes at Adelida.

"Who is Lewis?" Rueben asked.

"Your cousin," John said. "You and Lewis were here together. Your enlistment ended the same day. You were going home to a place you kept calling Love's Valley, Pennsylvania. Don't you even remember that? A little valley near a town called Shirleysburg."

"Afraid I don't," Rueben said. "I remember waking up from a knock on the head with blood all over my dear wife's skirt."

"Wife!" John Jacobs exclaimed. "What did you do last night? Lord Almighty! Lewis said if that woman he's been seeing would marry him, he'd stay in New Orleans, but you didn't mention getting married on the spur of the moment, too."

"Evidently that's what we both did," Rueben said. "Would you excuse us now, John? I'm sorry I don't remember you at all, and my head is pounding like a hammer."

"Then you are Mrs. Hamilton?" John eyed Adelida up and down rudely.

"You heard Rueben," Adelida said.

What had she just done? Rueben was a real Yankee. She should have known by the flat voice, but she'd been rattled to find her money all gone. Then there had been the robbery and that loud shotgun blast when the teller was killed. Blood all over her skirt. No wonder she didn't think about him being a Yankee. He was one of those despicable creatures from the North who'd killed all three of her brothers in the war, who'd caused her father to give up and die when he found his last son and favorite child had followed his other two brothers to an early grave. It's a wonder the sky didn't open up and fry her with big, bold lightning bolts for such blasphemy. The ship had already set sail and there was no way off it at this point, so she had no choice but to keep up the masquerade, but she sure didn't have to like it.

"I don't believe you," John whispered. "Lewis might marry on a whim, but not Rueben. He's a serious man and wouldn't marry a rebel. He was having trouble accepting the idea of his brother and cousin marrying rebels. Are you running some kind of scam?"

"Good day, Mr. Jacobs," she held her head high. "I don't have to explain anything to you."

"Captain Hamilton wouldn't marry you, not a Cajun," John stopped at the door and glared at her.

"John, you say we are friends. But even that doesn't give you the right to talk to my wife like that. You owe her an apology. This can't be easy for her either," Rueben said staunchly.

"My apologies." John nodded curtly toward Adelida.

"I'm going to sleep now. My head feels like it's filled with nothing but mud. Maybe when I awake, everything will be clear," Rueben said, as he stretched out on the bed.

Adelida nodded and with trembling hands continued to

unpack her trunk. She shook the wrinkles from the dresses and hung them in the armoire. She folded her petticoats, drawers and camisoles neatly and arranged them in
the drawers of the massive chest. She closed the trunk lid
and slid it over against the far wall, under the window.
Then she sank down in a plush, royal blue, velvet chair
and put her head in her hands.

"Such is life," she mumbled. And a crazy turn of life at
that. Three weeks ago she'd come to New Orleans to live
with her sister. Thoughts of Maria brought tears. She
wiped them away with the back of her hand. She wouldn't
let herself go to pieces again. She'd cried all night in the
Rue de Bateau for her sister. Now she had to keep her wits
about her. She kept the tears at bay, but she did remember
the past three weeks.

A month ago her father had died. Adelida, the youngest
child in the family, had taken care of her father for the
past six years, since she was fourteen. She'd watched him
go from a big, happy man to a withdrawn shadow of his
former self. Then she'd buried him beside her mother and
brothers in the church cemetery.

Maria had invited her to New Orleans when she sold
the bateau. She groaned as she thought of the family
bateau, her father's boat. The money from selling it had
all been spent in less than a month for pretty dresses, hats
and underthings. What could she have been thinking?
Had she kept the money, she wouldn't be in her current
predicament. On the other hand, Victor probably would
have taken it all anyway.

Rage renewed, she paced the floor. She'd had three
weeks with her sister—shopping, arguing, fighting, trying
to understand how someone with Broussau blood flowing
in her veins could really love Victor. Then a stray bullet

from a duel had found Maria's heart, killing her instantly. The next morning, Victor had evicted Adelida, telling her he wasn't having a southern Cajun in his home. It would ruin his reputation. When she'd reminded him that his wife came from the same family as she, he'd slapped her and screamed that he and Maria had come up in the world and he wouldn't be dragged back down by the likes of Adelida.

Memories played out, she sat on the top of her trunk and watched the land disappear slowly as the ship traveled out to sea. Perhaps she should do something constructive, like play the part of a good wife and unpack Rueben's trunk. The worst thing she'd find in there would be his unmentionables, and she'd done washing for three brothers and her father as long as she could remember, so that wouldn't be any big deal. Inside his wallet she found so much money, it staggered her imagination.

She folded his shirts neatly and laid them in the drawer. In another drawer, she stored his handkerchiefs, cuff links, extra collars and socks, and she hung his trousers in the armoire beside her own dresses. By all appearances, they were a married couple sharing a chest of drawers and an armoire.

When she reached the bottom of the trunk, she discovered a packet of letters tied with a piece of twine. Most of them were addressed to Captain Henry Rueben Hamilton and posted in a place called Shirleysburg, Pennsylvania. A few were addressed to the same but sent from Savannah, Georgia. She laid them on the desk and stared at them for a full ten minutes. They were his very personal property and she had no right, none whatsoever, to read them. However, if they contained information she could pass on, that would help him regain his memories.

She untied the string and picked up the first one.

Maybe he already had a wife and the letters were from her. Now, wouldn't that create a tempest in a tea cup! If Adelida found out the man she was married to had been living in a fancy stateroom with another woman, she'd throw a fit. Some things were unforgivable. With shaking hands she opened the first envelope. She flipped through three pages to the end to find that it was from someone who signed it as his sister, Indigo. She went back to the first page. The handwriting was lovely. Perfect. The tone of the letter was the opposite.

Evidently, Indigo was engaged to a man named Tommy and planned to marry in the early fall. She was glad Rueben would be home for the wedding and was also glad the two of them had enough sense not to marry rebels. It seemed her other brother had brought a sassy Texas woman home with him and married her. The Texan had a man's name, Douglass, and Indigo hated her even if she did make Monroe happy. Then their cousin had married Douglass' brother, Colum, and they were building a home in Love's Valley.

A letter from Rueben's mother, Laura, was a lot softer. She adored Douglass and Colum and was glad both Monroe and Ellie had found someone to share their lives with. Laura missed her sons and would be glad when Rueben and Reed were home this summer. It would be wonderful for the whole family to attend Indigo's wedding in the last part of August.

A letter from Monroe told Rueben about the valley, the horses, the new house he and Douglass had just moved into, Ellie and Colum's wedding, and how much he looked forward to help in the valley.

She laid aside the letters she'd read. Great goodness, these people must be richer than Midas to own a whole valley. When she had been a child, Adelida had told her family she was going to grow up and move far away into the mountains where the air was cool, where there was land under her feet all the time, and where she could hang clothing on a line instead of the edge of the bateau's rails. Her brothers and father had told her she was born on the bayou and she'd die on it. Her cousins had laughed at her, and she'd hidden in the bateau the rest of the day, declaring the whole time she would indeed make the journey some day.

And I will, but it won't be with a Yankee, she thought as she picked up the last letter and opened it. It was from his brother Reed, who was stationed in Savannah and would be watching the ship schedules so he could spend a few hours with him when The *Queen* docked in Savannah.

She picked up a piece of ship stationary from the desk and wrote: *Indigo, sister. Monroe and Reed, brothers. Laura, mother. Douglass, sister-in-law, married to Monroe. Ellie, cousin married to Colum, Douglass' brother. One sister. One female cousin. Two brothers.*

They all lived in Love's Valley or would be living there when the two younger brothers, Rueben and Reed, got home. For the next fifteen minutes she committed all of it to memory. Then she ripped the paper into confetti-sized pieces and carefully transferred them to the pocket of her oldest dress in the armoire.

"Mmmmm," Rueben awakened slowly from a dream where he was reaching out to someone just ahead of him in a dense, gray fog.

"Are you awake?" Adelida asked from the chair where she'd silently recited the names of his family.

"Yes, where are we?" he asked. The woman with the thick, black hair and perfectly arched eyebrows over big, round, ebony-colored eyes was his wife. He remembered that much. They'd been in a bank and he had tried to prevent a robbery, but he didn't remember any of it.

"We're on *The Queen*, a ship taking us to Baltimore, Maryland. From there we will go to Pennsylvania to your home in the mountains. A place called Love's Valley," she told him.

"Do I have family there?" He sat up, holding his head. It felt like one big bruise, but at least the pounding had ceased while he had slept.

"Yes, Rueben, you do. Your mother, Laura, lives there. Your sister, Indigo. Remember her? She's engaged to a fellow named Tommy. And your brother Monroe, and his new wife, Douglass."

"That's not a woman's name," Rueben drew his eyebrows down in a rigid frown.

"I agree, but I didn't name the girl. She's a Texan, remember?"

"No, I don't. I know where Texas is and I remember something about someone going there," he said. "But I don't remember any brothers or a sister. What did you say her name is?"

"Your sister is Indigo. A pretty name for a lady," Adelida said. *For a Yankee woman, that is. No self-respecting southern woman would name her baby girl such a silly name.*

"I suppose," Rueben said.

"And you have a brother in Savannah who is going to meet our bateau when we dock there," she said. "Won't that be a surprise for him when he finds out you are married?"

"What's his name?" Rueben asked.

"Harry Reed," she said. "Did you call him Harry Reed or just one or the other?"

"I wouldn't know," Rueben said. "I just know that I'm hungry. Could we go to the dining room?"

"No, not today. I'll go and put in an order to have it

brought to us in our room. I do think it best that we take our meals in here, and you stay in bed for a couple of days," she told him.

"I'll go stark raving mad," he said, swinging his legs over the side of the bed. Everything spun in violent circles. "Wooooo," he braced himself with his hands.

"See, you are not ready to stand or walk yet," she crossed the room in a hurry and grabbed his shoulders, forcing him back into the safety of the bed. "I'm going to undress you and help you get beneath the covers. It's already mid-afternoon, so resting until tonight shouldn't be a hardship," she talked, as she removed his boots and socks and then unbuckled his belt. What an experience. Undressing a fine looking man down to his shorts, all the time wishing she could pick up a pillow and smother him to death simply for being a Yankee.

"Okay," he agreed. "When did I tell you all about my family?"

"Rueben, we've been in love for three weeks. You've talked of nothing but your family and going home to Love's Valley. Your memory will come back if you rest. I'm from the Bayou Penchant. Remember? You and I met at the theater that first night I was in town. It was love at first sight," she swallowed hard on that lie. She'd never love a miserable Yankee, not even a half addled one who would take her far away from Victor LaSalle and his threats.

"And we married last night?" he asked. The room stopped moving when he was flat on his back. Adelida undressed him, so she had to be his wife, but surely he would remember something about her. Even a brain as sick as his wouldn't forget marrying a beautiful woman.

"Yes, we decided to marry on the spur of the moment so I could go home with you to Love's Valley. We were in love, and you were going to return to New Orleans for me in a few months anyway. We just married sooner, that's all," she said, helping him roll to one side so she could turn down the covers and get him tucked in.

It had the ring of truth to it, he thought. He did remember drinking champagne and someone toasting him over and over again. But a Cajun? Doubts tried hard to surface. Why wouldn't he want to be married to a Cajun, he wondered. Or perhaps it wasn't him at all, but his family who would be scandalized by his sudden marriage.

"What would you like to eat?" she asked.

"I don't know. Evidently you know me better than I do, so you order for both of us," he said, staring blankly at the ceiling.

"Then I will do that," she said, hoping that she didn't make the wrong choice. "Maybe something bland until we see if you are going to be sick when you eat."

"Fish," he said. "Fried with potatoes and no rice." Now where had that come from? He didn't know what he liked or didn't like, and suddenly out of the far reaches of his blank mind he'd found something.

"Then fish it shall be," she smiled, leaning forward to kiss him on the forehead.

She wiped her mouth vigorously on the way to the door.

Chapter Three

Lifting his glass of champagne high for a toast, Rueben drew his new bride close to his side. She fit in the crook of his arm perfectly and their hearts beat in unison, one beat, one life forever. Then suddenly she pulled away from him and disappeared into the crowd of happy relatives. Adelida had stepped into his life three weeks before and Rueben had married her. He tossed back the glass of champagne and someone refilled it for him. Where was his wife? She should be beside him. Panic filled his chest. She was gone and he didn't know where to go without her.

Rueben awoke with a start, sitting straight up in his bed, covers shoved to the floor, a cool ocean breeze flowing through the open port hole, sweat beading up on his forehead. Raising an imaginary glass to his lips, he realized he'd been dreaming. But it had been so real. Especially the fear of losing Adelida. One quick glance across a short span of no more than three feet proved she was sleeping soundly in her own bed. Why was she in that bed and not cuddled up beside him?

The doctor said we can't sleep together until you can

remember. It might be taxing on your brain, her words came back to haunt him. He argued with himself that it couldn't hurt to simply snuggle up next to her. Perhaps the feel of her body next to his would bring back the past. He threw himself backwards onto the pillows and shut his eyes tightly. No amount of willing a memory could produce one. There was a wedding, a real one in a misty fog where he heard vows. The bride had long black hair and wore a lace veil. Then there was Adelida holding his head in her lap while the doctor said something about a concussion. A friend, John Jacobs, had come by the stateroom and visited, and doubted that Adelida was his wife. He'd told Rueben that they'd been in the military together, but Rueben had absolutely no recollection of such a thing.

When nothing came to him, he rolled over to one side, drew the covers around his chest, and drank in the sight of his wife in the next bed. Clouds shifted back and forth across the moon, its rays forming a lace pattern over Adelida. She was so beautiful it took his breath away. Long black hair framed a delicate face carved from the purest porcelain. Dark lashes rested serenely on her cheeks. A full mouth was there, made for kissing. Both hands were together in a little girl's prayer position but tucked under her cheek instead of in front of her face.

Still awake at dawn, he eased out of bed and opened his trunk for a fresh shirt. It was empty; like his poor brain, there was nothing there. Adelida must have unpacked for him. Everything she did or said pointed to the fact that they were married, yet Rueben didn't feel married. He just felt an enormous relief that Adelida knew where he was going and was taking him there. He prowled through the chest, finding her underthings in the top drawer and his shirts near the bottom, along with fresh collars. The armoire door squeaked slightly, but didn't wake Adelida.

He checked his reflection in the mirror. He would shave and remove that ridiculous bandage. He found his knife amongst the things she'd removed from his pocket and carefully sliced through the white fabric. Then he leaned close to the mirror and examined the hole in his forehead. It appeared to be healing well. There were no red streaks shooting out from the stitches. How could a small wound like that erase so much? Using the fancy washcloth next to the basin, he dampened his dark brown hair, combing it all straight back. Closer scrutiny in the mirror revealed no bruise, just stitches and a blank brain.

He sharpened his razor and then began removing a heavy stubble. So he had a couple of brothers and they lived in Pennsylvania. Their names were Monroe and Harry Reed and he had a sister, Indigo. He wondered what they looked like. Did his brothers have the same slight cleft in their chins that gave them misery when they shaved? Where was his father? Adelida mentioned a mother, but no father. Was he dead? More questions that had no answers. He dried his face, pressed the washcloth against a nick to stop the bubble of blood, and put on a fresh collar.

The smell of coffee wafting across the dining room greeted him when he opened the door. Waiters bustled around, setting the round tables for breakfast. His nose followed the delicious aroma to a table in the corner where an urn awaited. Two other men already had cups in their hands, and Rueben could hear the soft buzz of their conversation as he headed in that direction.

"Rueben," John greeted him with a nod. "Are you better this morning?"

"The headache is gone, but I do think I could use a cup of that coffee," Rueben said.

John filled a cup and handed it to him. "And have you remembered marrying that woman?"

"Can't say as I remember anything other than a wedding and waking up with my head in her lap after a bank robbery," he said.

"Well, I bought a newspaper yesterday afternoon when we stopped to unload cargo and pick up the mail," John told him. "It had news of that robbery right on the second page. Just a small article that said one teller had been killed and another man was injured, but he and his wife were able to continue on with their plans. I suppose I was wrong, but it sure doesn't seem right. You were so adamant about Lewis courting that Southern woman. He had to really talk hard to get you to say you'd stand with him if he married her at the last minute. You told him emphatically that someday the South and North might mix again but not in this generation, not after the war we just fought."

"Guess I was wrong," Rueben sipped the coffee. Nothing had ever tasted so good. Not even morning coffee in the bivouacs during the war. "I was in a war," he whispered. "What war?"

"The War between the States," John said. "So you are beginning to get something back, my friend. That's good. Maybe by the time I get off this ship, you will remember everything."

"I just caught a glimpse of a campsite with men all around in uniforms. We were drinking coffee and the sun was coming up. It was going to be another hot, stuffy day," Rueben said, elated at the memory.

Adelida awoke slowly, letting her mind adjust to the gentle rocking of the ship before she opened her eyes. With every mile she was getting farther away from New Orleans. But with every mile there was the possibility Rueben would instantly remember everything. Yet, even if he put her out on the very next dock, she wouldn't be a bit farther behind than she'd been. She'd still be penniless and have to find something to keep body and soul together, but she'd be out of Louisiana. The warmth of the morning sneaking through the port hole onto her face finally forced her eyes open.

Today her sister Maria would be buried in New Orleans. Adelida should be there for the funeral, wearing a black dress and mourning. By rights, she should be wearing black for a year for her father, but Maria had declared that to be a silly old notion and insisted she buy pretty things. It hadn't been so hard to convince Adelida to do just that. For the first time in her twenty years there had been money to buy pretty frocks.

Fully awake, a new day dawning, she figured she'd better arise, get dressed and go order breakfast. She really needed to convince Rueben to stay in today anyway. John Jacobs would be home by this time tomorrow and it would be safer to let Rueben wander about after that. She moved the pillow blocking the view of the other bed to see if Rueben was still sleeping or if he was staring off into space like he did when his eyes were open. Poor man. Yankee or not, it would be horrible to lose your memory, to have to depend on someone you didn't even know to take care of you. She'd do that for sure. She owed him that much, no matter if he'd taken the wrong side of the war.

Rueben's bed was empty, the armoire door stood open, and two drawers in the chest weren't shut quite all the way. She sat up with a start, just knowing that he'd awakened with a full memory and had hurriedly dressed to go bring the ship's captain to arrest her. Did they have a jail on this magnificent ship? Would they really put a her in it? What would happen now?

She threw off her night rail with no thought of Rueben

or the ship's captain rushing in. In ten minutes she was dressed from the skin out in lace trimmed drawers, a matching camisole, two petticoats, and shirtwaist of a lighter blue than the dark blue traveling suit with a matching skirt and fitted jacket. She wound her hair into a loose bun at the nape of her neck, secured it there with pins, and set a small hat on top of her head. At least she looked like a lady even if she felt like a criminal.

The friendly aroma of breakfast greeted her when she opened the door. She scanned the dining room, filled with pockets of men, women, and children, some already seated, others still visiting. She located Rueben beside the coffee table, visiting with John and another man. His bandages had been removed and his hair was combed back like it was the previous morning when she had landed flat on her back and looked up into the most handsome face she'd ever seen.

Rueben looked across the room, a quizzical expression on his face as he waved to her.

She waved back. The look on Rueben's face terrified her, but she'd wait to fall to pieces until she knew for sure that she'd been found out. From the sour expression on John Jacob's face, it was going to be a swim or drown situation. Well, she wouldn't go down without a good old Broussau fight.

"Good morning, gentlemen," she held her head high and gazed into Rueben's brown eyes, trying to find an answer.

"Adelida," Rueben nodded. Was he supposed to touch her arm or pat her shoulder? What did married men do with wives in public? "Did you sleep well?" he asked, using one hand to hold the saucer under the coffee cup and the other to lift the coffee to his mouth. With both hands occupied, he couldn't be expected to touch her.

"Of course," she said. "I love the night breezes, so I opened the window. It wasn't too much air for you, I hope."

"Not at all," Rueben said. "Gentlemen, this is my wife, Adelida Hamilton. Adelida, you've met John. This is his friend, Russell Pacton. They've been telling me things about myself. I was Captain Hamilton in the military and stationed in the South to help with the reconstruction after the war. I did remember something this morning. A campsite and soldiers. Isn't that wonderful, Adelida?"

"Of course, dear, shall we find a table for breakfast?" She looped her arm in his, hoping the other two men would discreetly fade away. He hadn't remembered. Not yet, anyway. And they hadn't convinced him he wasn't married.

She had a while longer before he looked at her and began to scream she wasn't his wife but some kind of con artist—which she was.

"Join us," he motioned to his two new friends. "John, tell me more. I swear it's the strangest thing to be in this shape."

"I'm sure they have their own families to attend to," she said softly.

"Not at all," John said. "I'm a bachelor like Rueben was until a couple of days ago. I'd be most glad to join you."

Adelida shot him a look meant to drop him stone cold dead on the spot. He merely raised an eyebrow and smiled brightly.

The bacon was fried crisp, exactly the way she liked, and the eggs were scrambled in butter in a fluffy mound. Pancakes were no bigger than a silver dollar, but drenched in maple syrup. At any other time and place, Adelida would have eaten like a fisherman who'd been out all day on the bayou, but it was nothing more than something to nibble on while her stomach tightened up. She listened to John tell stories about the war until she wanted to use her butter knife to carve his heart out and throw it over the side of the ship to the hungry fish. But she nodded at the appropriate times, patted Rueben's arm when he laughed at a story, and sipped her coffee, too weak by any self-respecting Cajun standards, but at least it was hot and black.

"I can't remember one thing you've mentioned. And the worst of it is, I can remember only vaguely being at a wedding. It's as if I was at someone else's marriage ceremony and not my own," Rueben shook his head.

"Oh, but you'll remember. When your brain has time to heal, then you will remember," Adelida patted his hand.

"Of course I will. It's just so confusing," Rueben said. "John says that I've shunned Southern women with a passion. Then, suddenly, I am married to one?"

"And you believe this buffoon over your wife, the one you stood before a priest and said you would love and honor until death parted you from me? How do you know he's not lying to you? Tell me that, if you can," she said, wishing for all the world that she could take the words back the minute they were out in the open. Fighting was as common to her as breathing, and her father had told her time and time again that the hardest lesson she would ever learn was when to keep her mouth shut. But she was tired of being doubted, even if she was lying.

"John is my friend," Rueben said tightly. "You are embarrassing me in public. Apologize to him."

"I will not," Adelida tossed her napkin on the table.

"It's not necessary," John said graciously. "If I were in her shoes, I'd most likely feel the same way about me."

Red hot glares from both Rueben and Adelida met somewhere in the distance between them and ignited into a fireworks display only the two of them could see. She wouldn't apologize if it meant diving overboard and swimming back up the Mississippi Sound, around Cat Island and across the Borgne Lake to the shores of New Orleans. How dare he insult her in front of other people! If this was the way the Yankees treated their women, it was a wonder there were people left in the North. The whole race should have expired years before the war.

Rueben was not going to tolerate such behavior from his wife. It was uncalled for and unacceptable. She would apologize or they'd have worse words when they got back to their room. He'd never liked overbearing, rude women, so why had he married one? If only he could regain what he'd lost, he might have an answer to that.

"Well?" he said in a tone guaranteed to turn the ocean into one big chunk of ice.

"Well, what? I said it and I'll stand by it," she said, her voice so cold as to make his seem warm in comparison.

"Apologize," he said tightly.

"If you don't believe we are truly married, then put me off the bateau at the next stop. Give me enough money so I can go back home to the Bayou Penchant. There's lots of cousins who will take me in, I'm sure. Then when you get your mind back, you can wish I was with you," she said just above a whisper, her flashing, dark eyes never leaving his.

"Only a wife would argue with a man like that," John laughed, breaking the tension. "Honeymoon jitters plus a husband with amnesia. No wonder you're arguing."

"Adelida?" Rueben pushed the issue.

"No," she said. "This is war. The battle lines are drawn. Put me off the boat or don't doubt me. Why would a fine, southern Cajun woman be willing to go north to your Yankee home if she did not love you with her whole heart?"

"Point well spoken," John said. "I surrender. I lay down my sword and my guns, Mrs. Hamilton. Touché. You have made a believer out of me. Rueben, I think you'd better be thanking your stars for this woman. Looks like she'd fight a forest fire with a cup of water to keep her new marriage intact. I'm just glad she wasn't allowed to join the troops in the war or it might have turned out different."

"To be sure it would. If you hardheaded men with blood in your eyes would have consulted your mothers and sisters, your wives and daughters, there would have been no war. We would have settled it without bloodshed, most likely over a cup of good black coffee and beignets," she said. "Now, will you please excuse me? I'm going to walk on the deck before the storm hits and then go to my room."

"What storm?" Russell asked.

"There's a storm brewing. A bayou Cajun knows when it's going to storm. Something about the wind and the smell in the air. The wind has already begun to pick up. It might be today or tomorrow, but it won't be long," she said. "Don't stand. Enjoy the rest of your breakfast, gentlemen. Perhaps we'll have lunch together, and you can refresh Rueben's mind even more."

Chapter Four

Adelida leaned on the back of the door into the state-room until she caught her breath and willed her heart to quit trying to jump from her breast out onto the floor. If Rueben had called her bluff, she'd be 'gater bait for sure by now. John Jacobs had been lying through his teeth when he'd buried the hatchet and called a truce. His words and his eyes did not match. She paced the floor, attempting to shake off the antsy feeling tensing every muscle in her body. Sticking her head out the still open porthole she inhaled the salty air. Clouds gathered on the horizon and a stiff wind had picked up. A storm was brewing, but it was nothing compared to the one down deep inside her. She might have won one tiny battle, but it didn't mean she'd won the war.

Married! Adelida didn't know one thing about being a wife. She knew how to fish, how to keep house on a small house bateau. She knew how to cook and do laundry, survive on what the bayou offered when there was no money after the war. When others were starving, the Broussau

family had at least eaten well. They had owned no land,
never had; they'd farmed a small plot her father leased
from a sugar plantation owner. The vegetable garden produced what they could not take from the bayou. To pay for
the lease, he used his bateau at harvest time to take sugar
from the dock to Houma.

By now, most of Adelida's cousins had already been
married for four or five years, some even six or seven.
They had families and ran their bateaus with the grace of
women who lived in big, fancy houses.

"Something wrong?" John Jacobs asked from not three
feet from her on the other side of the small window.

"Where's Rueben?"

"He's sitting on the deck enjoying the lovely morning.
Strange. One would think a new wife would be sitting
with him instead of sulking about in her room. Of course,
if she was indeed his wife," he tipped his hat, leaving her
speechless.

She'd been right. Mr. Jacobs had merely pretended to
believe her. Thank goodness he'd be getting off the ship
later that day. She'd have to be extra careful until then.
She pinched her pale cheeks to give them some color,
tucked a strand of black hair into her chaste bun, and went
off to find Rueben, to pretend to be something she would
never be—the wife of a Yankee military officer.

"Ah, my new wife joins me," Rueben patted the chaise
lounge next to his side. "It is wonderful not to have a
headache this fine morning. Tell me again, Adelida, what
did I do to warrant such a brutal hit on my head?"

"You tried to single-handedly stop a bank robbery," she
arranged her skirts discreetly so no ankle showed. "The
bandit said for you to come to the middle of the bank and
sit with me where I waited for you. When you got there,

you reached inside your jacket to pull out a gun. The robber hit you on the head. One of the others shot a teller in the chest with a shotgun."

"I see," he said. "I'm sorry to keep asking you the same questions. I just think surely some little detail will jar my memory back into existence. It's bewildering to be in this condition. I'm just glad you are here and know where we are going. I promise to make it all up to you when things are right. This can't be much of a honeymoon for you."

"Are you still mad at me for not apologizing to that overbearing friend of yours?" she asked.

"Of course I am, but you'll make it up to me later," he said, with a twinkle in his eye. "We're supposed to fight so we can kiss and make up at the end of the day. Isn't that what newlyweds do on their honeymoon? And I'm sitting here thinking about how nice that's going to be."

"The doctor said—" she gasped, wide-eyed with panic.

"I know what the doctor said. You told me when you put me to bed last night. I do remember everything you've said since yesterday morning. But that doesn't mean we can't kiss and make up, does it? You are my wife, Adelida. And kissing is part of marriage. All day long, I shall look forward to cuddling with you and kissing you until you are breathless. The anticipation of claiming those pretty lips for my own will make it even better when the time comes."

She'd have to let him kiss her even if he was a Yankee. There was no way out of that, but she'd slit her wrists and be thrown to rot under a cypress tree in the bayou before she did one thing more. She'd shared a few awkward kisses in the shadows of a barn dance in her lifetime, so she wasn't totally innocent. She just hoped her lips didn't rot off after she kissed him.

In spite of her sassiness, she was in a complete state of

shock. She'd exchanged one problem for another. Victor had threatened her and scared the devil out of her. But now she'd ruined her reputation by traveling unchaperoned with Rueben, by sleeping in the same room with him, by undressing him down to his shorts for bed. Death or loss of dignity. She'd chosen the latter and she'd have to live with the consequences.

The ship slowed and turned, land appearing ahead of them. Adelida thought seriously of ending the charade right then and there. But she just couldn't make herself do it. Perhaps if her Cajun luck held she would make it all the way to those mountains in Pennsylvania and just for one day smell that fresh mountain air. The anxiety attacks along the journey to reach that vision would be worth it. Until then she would endure what she had to.

Up to a point.

"Ah, land. Where are we?" Rueben combed his thick, dark hair back with his fingers and covered a yawn with the other hand.

"I have no idea," Adelida said.

"We are coming into Fort Morgan," a steward rounded the end of the row of lounges. "I'm to let everyone know in case they want to get off and walk on solid ground for a while. We will unload cargo here and pick up mail. We'll be in port two hours. Then this afternoon we will dock again at four o'clock if all goes well. We are suggesting that all passengers take advantage of the time since today will be the last chance to get off the ship for many days."

"Thank you," Rueben said. "Well, my dear, shall we go back to the cabin and ready ourselves for a couple of hours on dry land?"

"Of course," Adelida said, already thinking that she'd have to change her shoes into something more comfortable. She didn't suppose it would be proper to walk around Fort Morgan in her bare feet like she did on the bayou where she'd known everyone who had lived there for the past three generations.

Rueben watched his new wife tuck back a few strangling strands of long, jet black hair into the bun at the nape of her neck. He longed to slowly remove every one of the pins holding that massive hair in place and tangle his hands in it, just letting the silky mane flow through his fingers. But that would have to be later when everything was right again. The doctor had warned them they could not live as a married couple until he had full use of his damaged brain again. The impression Adelida gave him was that it could be fatal.

Ah, but what a way to go, he thought, the idea bringing a grin to his face.

"Much more primping and we shall miss our opportunity to get off the ship," he teased.

"I'm ready," she snapped, her black eyes cutting across the room in an attempt to chill him to the bone.

She did have a snappy way about her when she was angry. Surely he hadn't thought he was choosing a soft natured, patient woman. If he had, when he came out of his dose of memory loss, he was surely going to be disappointed. "Then let's go, Mrs. Hamilton. Do you know anything about Fort Morgan?"

"Not one thing," she said. "I could give you a fine tour of Bayou Penchant and a very brief one of New Orleans, but those are the only places I'm familiar with."

He held out his arm, and she had no recourse but to take it. Her cousins in the bayou would shun her forever and possibly string her up from the nearest cypress tree for consorting with the enemy. Even if the war was over, they were still the enemy. At least Louisiana could be reconstructed and resettled without the arrogant Yankees com-

ing back into the bayous. They might find a whole different reception there than they'd found in the big cities.

Fort Morgan was nothing like what Adelida expected.
After the fancy ship, she'd somehow thought the streets
would be paved with gold bricks at every port where it
would drop anchor, but Fort Morgan was exactly what its
name implied—a military fort. There were more than a
hundred people who'd opted to get off *The Queen* that
hot, humid morning, strolling through the streets of a
working fort, some visiting the chapel for a few quiet
moments of meditation, but most using their time to shop
in the small general store.

Rueben and Adelida skipped the chapel and went
straight into the store. He looked at small handguns. She
fingered the pretty fabric and laces.

"Well, my dear, what can we buy for you today?"
Rueben asked.

The idea that he would spend money on her took her
aback. There was nothing she needed. She had plenty of
dresses, thanks to her sister's impulsive buying. What she
needed was her reputation back and that couldn't be
bought in a fort's general store.

He reached out and ran his forefinger down the angle of
her jaw and across her full, sensuous mouth. He really did
look forward to kissing those lips tonight after supper.
Perhaps he could talk her into sleeping with him, even if
that's all they did.

So hot was the trail where his fingertips had been, he
might as well have touched her with a hot coal. She stood
there addled even more than she'd been the night Maria
crumbled in a heap just outside the theater or when the
teller told her there was absolutely no money in her
account.

Rueben liked the high color filling his new wife's

cheeks. He picked up her left hand, bringing it to his lips to plant a sweet kiss on her tender palm. "Ah, I know what we shall buy for my new wife. I see that in our hurry to marry, we did not buy you a wedding ring. If the man has one, that's what we'll purchase."

Her knees were rubbery after he kissed her hand. She nodded sweetly and wondered what on earth she would do with a gold wedding ring when he found out she wasn't his wife.

"Could we see your wedding rings?" Rueben led her to the counter. "We were married quite hastily a couple of days ago. In the middle of the night. And this is the first opportunity I've had to buy my wife a ring."

The man pulled out a tray of rings and set them before Rueben and Adelida. "I've only got the plain ones," he apologized.

"That will do until we get home," Rueben picked up the widest gold band in the case and held it out to Adelida. "Try this one for size."

It fit perfectly and felt as if it would burn a circle on her finger. "Thank you," she managed to whisper.

"My pleasure," Rueben leaned over and kissed the ring, then her palm again and finished with a lingering kiss on her cheek.

She burned with complete shame. She'd duped the man. Shutting her eyes to draw enough courage to give the ring back before he could pay for it, she saw only green trees growing on mountains. She opened her eyes, held up the new, shiny ring to catch the sun rays filtering through the general store's only window, and smiled at Rueben.

"Something seems familiar about this place," Rueben said. "Like I've been here before."

"Where you from?" The man made change from the money Rueben handed him.

"Pennsylvania. Served in the war with the Union," he said.

"I'm from New York. Sent down here to hold the fort together after the war was over," the man told him. "We took possession of Fort Morgan in the spring of 1864, about a year before the war ended. Did you fight in this area?"

"Yes, I did," Rueben said. "I was with the troops that brought Fort Morgan into Union possession, and I just remembered that. You see, I was hit in the head during a bank robbery a couple of days ago and my memory was gone when I awoke. But this morning I remembered the smell of coffee around a campfire with soldiers around me. And now I remember it was during the battle of Mobile Bay. So I suppose my memory is going to return by little spurts."

Adelida held her breath until she thought she might pass out on the wooden floor of the Fort Morgan general store. The doctor said it could come in bits and pieces or as a whole rushing dam. "So is that all you can remember?" she asked.

"For now," Rueben said. "It feels good to just get a little bit every now and then. But I do recollect that battle and the men around me that early spring morning. Even though it was April, it was already hot and sticky and the mosquitoes were big as buzzards."

The man behind the counter chuckled. "And they still are. I hate mosquitoes. I hate this humid heat, but most of all I hate the tropical storms. We haven't had one yet this year and everyone keeps saying there's a feel in the air that one is on the way."

Adelida nodded. "If you've been raised around water, you can feel it in the air."

"Don't tell me that," the man rolled his eyes. "And let's hope you are wrong, lady. Because you'll be out there on the high seas for three days after this stop. There's at least one boat wreck down in the area you'll be in by then. Folks make their living working the wrecks and selling the goods they find."

"Everything would be wet and waterlogged," Adelida said.

"It'll dry out and some things are only improved by a good washing," the man said. "You're not from the north, are you?"

"Louisiana," she said.

"Well, you two got your jobs cut out for you. You are taking a rebel wife home to Pennsylvania right after the war?" The man looked seriously at Rueben.

"Yes, I am," Rueben said. "But love conquers everything. I'm just grateful to remember that battle and have a bit of my past back. Maybe by the time we get home, I'll remember everything."

"That would be a good thing," the man said. "If I took a rebel wife home, my mother would shoot her then turn the gun on me. She'd never accept such a woman. Not after losing three of her sons to the war. No offense meant to you personally, ma'am."

"I lost all three of my brothers to the war," Adelida said shortly. "My cousins would draw and quarter Rueben Hamilton, then feed him to the gaters in the swamp if I took him home to the Bayou Penchant."

A deep chill worked its way up Rueben's spine. Her voice held the absolute vibration of truth in it. She came from that backwoods area known as Acadia. The men at the base in New Orleans said they'd rather fight another war than be lost back in that part of Louisiana. The only Yankees that ever went back there stayed. Not because of the fine southern hospitality, but because they never lived to see the light of another day. The Acadians were fiercely loyal to their families and their beliefs, neither of which welcomed anyone from the North into its bosom. This new memory he didn't share with either the soldier behind the counter or his new wife.

"I'm very sorry," the man said honestly to Adelida. "Given that bit of information, I shall stay out of Louisiana."

"I do apologize for my quick temper. Why, I do believe our time is about gone. Thank you so much for jarring my dear husband's mind into remembrance," she said, looping her arm through Rueben's and practically dragging him out of the store.

"That was refreshing," he said. "Now you are marked, my lovely bride. Everyone will know we are married."

"Yes, they will," she whispered, all the fight gone from her.

Chapter Five

Adelida appeared from behind the hinged screen with a shawl tucked tightly around her shoulders. It covered a worn night rail, so different from the fancy dress she'd worn that day. An irritating idea that the outside and inside of his new wife were mismatched plagued Rueben. One minute she was sass and brass, flipping her fancy skirttails around; the next she was soft and demure, almost shy, in a sleeping gown that had seen better days.

"Sit down and let me brush your hair," he motioned toward the vanity bench covered in burgundy velvet.

"I can do my own hair. You know what the doctor said," she protested, drawing her shawl even tighter, clenching it until her knuckles were white.

"I know what the doctor said. You keep reminding me," he ran the back of his hand down her soft cheek, stopping to gently cup her chin in his hand and look deeply into ebony eyes still popped wide open. "Maybe he was wrong, Adelida. Maybe sleeping with you would jar my memory." Rueben looked away from her wide eyes and down at the brush she'd laid on the vanity. It was a plain one with a wooden handle, and contradicted the fancy-dressed woman he had spent time with in the daylight hours. Just who was Adelida Broussau anyway?

"We're not taking that chance," she said, and sat down at the vanity. It was wonderful to have something stable and secure under her. Just the mere touch of his hand on her face produced a weakness that practically had her leaning against him. If he wanted to brush her hair, then so be it. It seemed a bit on the strange side though. After all, it was just hair, and brushing it was as normal as eating. She'd never seen her father brush her mother's hair. It must be a Yankee thing and she didn't pretend to understand foreign customs.

"I'll do that," he gently pushed her hands away when she reached to take the pins out. "I've wanted to touch all this beautiful hair ever since I opened my eyes in the bank," he began the sensuous job of taking his wife's hair down. The long, ebony tresses filled his hands as the pins gave up their job. He combed through them with his fingertips. Pure desire flooded him at the touch of so much soft hair floating across his palms. If the mere touch of her hair could cause such sensations, he was sure sleeping with her would jar his memory immediately.

Every nerve in Adelida's body quivered when he raked his fingertips through her hair, his fingers feathering across the tender skin on her neck. She steeled herself for the next jolt when he actually began to brush her hair in long, lazy strokes. Two round hot spots flushed her cheeks. Pulsating vibrations turned her stomach into warm mush. Shivers crept up her backbone, settling in every pore on her head. She liked this foreign custom entirely too much. Conflicting emotions rattled through her. She wanted him to stop immediately, not liking the idea that any Yank could affect her like that. She also wanted him to never stop, never put the brush down, so great was the pleasure of a man's tender touch on her skin. She fought with her heart, reminding it that men like Rueben Hamilton had killed her brothers. In a far-fetched way, he was the reason her sister was dead also. If Victor LaSalle hadn't seen an opportunity to make money off the war, Maria wouldn't have been in New Orleans.

Her heart didn't listen.

"I wish I had an acre of hair like this to walk around in my bare feet on," he said, so close to her ear that the warmth of his breath gave her a whole new set of goosebumps.

"What a silly thing to say. It's just hair," she said breathlessly.

"Ah, but the softest, most sensuous hair I've ever seen," he whispered huskily. How could he be married to such a woman and not remember a single detail of their courtship? Had he ever touched her hair before? He couldn't remember, but he did most certainly look forward to the time when he could do more than just brush her hair, a time when she wouldn't sleep in a bed across the room from him.

Adelida took the brush from his hands and deftly braided her dark hair into two plaits. The infatuation had to die right then. She wouldn't take any more chances. From now on, she'd brush her hair while she was behind the dressing screen, coming out only when she was ready for bed. The way he'd made her feel when he touched her skin and kissed her neck left her weak and without a thread of dignity. From now on, she'd just have to be even more careful.

"Good night then, darling," Rueben laid his hands on her shoulders and turned her to face him.

She reached up to remove his hands, but he encased her

tiny hands in his oversized ones, drawing her palms to his chest. Slightly parted lips came closer and closer until they captured her mouth in a kiss. Bright colors reeled behind her closed eyelids. The bones in her legs turned into sap. Every thought between her ears, where her brain used to be, was engulfed with flames. It had to stop, but it was ecstasy while it lasted.

Finally she pulled back. Shaken to the bottom of her soul, she was glued to the floor, unable to move toward the bed.

"Good night," he murmured into her ear again, not wanting to end the moment. Desire begged him to forget what the doctor said and take his chances. One night with Adelida in his arms would be worth the risk.

"Good night," she said, surprised that she could utter a word.

She stumbled toward the bed and pulled the covers up around her neck. She wouldn't actually die from weak knees and tingles up her backbone, or even the flutters deep inside her stomach, when he touched her. But all of the feelings surely wouldn't let her sleep.

She flipped from one side of the bed to the other, listening to Rueben's soft breathing only a few feet away. Evidently, she hadn't affected him the way he had her or he wouldn't be able to sleep so soundly. She sighed, staring at the patterns of the moonbeams on the ceiling and living through a dozen or more scenarios when Rueben found his memory. Finally, unable to abide another minute of restlessness, she crawled out of bed, slipped behind the screen and redressed. She'd go to the upper deck and sit in the cool night air. She twisted the long braid around her head in a crown, securing it tightly with the pins on the vanity. It didn't matter if every hair wasn't perfect; she wouldn't see another soul anyway.

Easing the door open ever so quietly, she was surprised to see a few tables in the enormous dining area occupied with men playing cards. Cigar smoke, hanging heavily from eye-level to the ceiling, and the smell of bourbon made her nose twitch. It didn't take her long to push open the outside door and inhale the fresh night breeze. She made her way gingerly to the top deck. Big wheels on either side of the ship slurped through the water. Clouds moved across the stars and moon. A south wind whipped at her skirttail.

"Hello," a feminine voice startled Adelida when she sat down in one of the many empty lounge chairs. "What brought you out at this time of night?"

"Needed some fresh air," Adelida smoothed her skirt down as best she could.

"I'm Evangeline Morris," the woman said.

"Pleased to make your acquaintance," Adelida said. "I'm Adelida Broussau . . . Hamilton," she added.

"Newly married, huh? Still saying your maiden name out of habit. You'll get used to it. Took me a while the first time too. It gets easier with time," Evangeline said.

"I don't know if . . ."

"Well, I do. I married young like you back when I was sixteen. The war was going to be over in four months, so my sweetheart and I wed. I didn't have time to get used to his name before the Southern boys put a bullet between his eyes. I've been to the altar three times since then." Evangeline lit a cigar and puffed on it, the ember at the end glowing in the night.

Adelida was at a loss for words. "I'm sorry for your losses," she said softly.

"Oh, I didn't lose them all to the grave," Evangeline laughed loudly. "Lost one to jail for robbery, one to jail for murder, and the last one died for cheating at cards. But thank goodness he taught me the finer points of good poker before he got caught. I make my living now riding the ships up and down the coast playing poker. Three days up the coast and three back down. A week out of the month ain't bad for the style of living I'm accustomed to having."

"You play poker?" Adelida was amazed. "And you make money at it?"

"Honey, if I didn't I wouldn't be on this ship. Wouldn't make a good sailor at all. I sleep all day and play poker all night. It's a job. Just got bored with it tonight and began to let my mind wander. Did real good the last two nights. Tomorrow I'll be home on dry land for another month," Evangeline said. "My cigar doesn't bother you, does it? I could move on down the row a bit."

"No, not at all. I used to play a little poker with my brothers," Adelida said.

Evangeline smiled. "Well, what are you doing up here with me? With your looks you could clean up in the dining room right now. Just bat those pretty eyes and make them think you're bluffing. You really know how to play?"

"Some," Adelida said. She'd never thought of playing cards for real money. If she'd realized back in New Orleans that women could slide a chair up to a poker table, she wouldn't be wearing a wedding ring right then, nor would she have a pseudo-husband snoring in one of the best rooms on the ship.

"Here, honey," Evangeline stuck the cigar between her teeth and reached across the darkness.

"What is it?" Adelida asked cautiously.

"Well, it ain't cigar ashes. Should've never took up the habit. If you've a mind to play some poker, at least don't let them talk you into smoking with them. Oh, and if they offer to buy you a bourbon, let them. Even if you don't like it. Make sure you sit with your back to the wall, over there where the plants are located. Now me, I'm not adverse to sipping on a bourbon all evening. Like the cigars, I've grown to like the taste of good whiskey, but those silly men never know that one drink lasts me all night when I'm playing cards. Every time I catch them all studying their cards, I water the plants with the whiskey, leaving only a dribble in the bottom, which is what they see me drink. Works like a charm. Men seem to think they can get the woman drunk and show her that poker is for men," Evangeline put a stack of chips in Adelida's hand.

"That's enough to get you into a game. Go have a good time. I been very lucky on this trip. Or maybe I've just been playing with idiots," she puffed on the cigar.

"I couldn't," Adelida was glad for the darkness to cover the blush setting her face on fire.

"Yes, you can. I'm off to an early bed," Evangeline stood up and yawned. "Good luck. If it makes you feel any better you can give the money back to me if you win a lot. Don't know what it is you and your new husband have fought about tonight. Don't want to know. Just know from experience if you wasn't fighting you wouldn't be up here. You'd be all snuggled up in the crook of his arm. But a good game of poker will take your mind off whatever it was. If you ever played more than one game in your life, you know you got to keep your mind on the game, not on your troubles or what's for supper tomorrow night."

"Thank you," Adelida said.

"My pleasure. I played my first real game after my fourth husband bit the dust. I had a hundred dollars after I buried the low-down cheat. It was all the money I had in the world. When I walked away from that table at dawn the next morning, I had a thousand dollars. Hope you have the same luck. Don't let them put you in a tilt. They almost did me tonight. Damn near lost my stake. Play them close to the heart, Adelida, and don't let those rotten men push you to tears," she said.

"Why are you doing this? I'm a Louisiana woman. Southern. Your first husband?" Adelida asked.

"Looking back, I reckon it was all for the best. He was a sorry skunk. If you rebels hadn't shot him, I would have when he got home after what I found out about the worthless hunk of mankind. Saved me a prison term, way I figure it," Evangeline disappeared into the night.

Adelida stared at the handful of wooden chips. Could she do it? Just brazenly march into the dining room, draw up a chair, fake drinking whiskey and actually win money? If she even had a few dollars at dawn she could tell Rueben about the deception.

Resolutely she stiffened her spine, tucked her hair back into the braid crown and headed off toward the dining room again. The wind whipped her skirt around in a whirl around her ankles. There were no stars shining now, just big, black, angry clouds sending off blasts of warm, humid air. A storm was definitely brewing. She hoped they made it to port before it hit.

Opening the door to the smoke-filled room, she scanned the whole room. Two tables were still playing, one with ten players, all men, sipping whiskey and making small talk and the other, seven men with an empty chair at the table. Ignoring the fact that she was windblown and more than a little bit disheveled with strands of hair escaping her braid crown, she crossed the room and stood behind the empty chair.

"Mind if I sit in on this one?" she asked.

"What's a little Southern girl like you wanting to play

poker for? You and your new husband have a fight or something?" The big, pot-bellied dealer asked.

"How did you know I was a newlywed?" she asked.

"Seen you lots of times. Seen you sneak out of that room while ago and go topside. That's what women do when they fight. They run away and pout," he said.

"Some do," Adelida said.

"Sit right down, sugar. Voice like that tells me you're from the South. After listening to these old codgers all night, it'd be a pleasure to hear a sweet accent until you lose the chips in your hand." A tall, thin man with snow white hair pulled the chair out for her.

"Shouldn't take long," she smiled brightly. "What're ya'll biddin'?"

"No limit. Mostly ten, twenty and fifty. I'm Fred," the white-haired man said.

"Nice to meet you, Fred. Name is Adelida. From Louisiana," she sat down primly, sweeping her skirts to the side.

"You played before? Had a woman taking up that chair earlier this evening. She's quite the poker player. Damn near wiped me out," the big, burly man said without offering his name nor exchanging pleasantries.

"Played a little with my brothers before they were killed in the war," she admitted.

Big-burly laughed aloud. "Well, it won't take us long to steal those chips from you, lady. You sure you don't want to just take them over to the window and get your cash back for them?"

"Maybe I'll just try my luck a little. Going gets tough, I can always pull out and cash in what's left, right?" she asked.

"It's your option," Big-burly chuckled as he deftly

shuffled the deck and then made quite a show of giving each person five cards.

Adelida checked her hand. Two aces, one queen, a three and an eight. There was the possibility for three of a kind or a queen straight or perhaps two pair if a queen turned up. Big-burly grinned and drew deeply on his cigar, blowing perfect rings in the air above her head. He didn't have jack squat; she'd be willing to bet everything she had.

"What're you bettin'?" He turned to the man next to him.

"Startin' at ten," the man tossed his chips into the middle of the table.

The game began. Big-burly bluffed by blowing smoke rings. The man next to him pulled his ear. Baldy ran a finger down his crooked nose. Beady, she'd named for his squinty eyes, let his nostrils flare when he had a good hand and tended to reward himself with a slug of whiskey. Adelida named them all in her mind and watched them from the corner of her eye as she laid her bets on the table.

"Just me and you, little lady," Big-burly said after an hour of intense playing. "And me, I think you're bluffing," he blew a perfect smoke ring at her. It settled on top of her black hair like a misty, gray halo.

"Could be," she rubbed her wedding ring. It was as good a ploy as any. Didn't matter what she did, if she could convince him she was bluffing, then she had the upper hand, because she was holding three aces and two kings. A full house on a boat.

"I've got three of a kind," Big-burly laid three fours, a jack and a ten on the table.

"Fred, I think this might beat that. Am I right?" She spread her cards on the table.

"I reckon you would be right at that," Fred raked all the chips to her place. "Want to go another hand and let us see if we could win back part of that pile?"

"I don't know. I should just cash them in," Adelida said softly. "Maybe I'm over my mad spell now."

"Oh, no, you don't, lady," Big-burly shook his head. "You don't sit down here with beginner's luck and rob us all blind. You'll stay for at least another round."

"Well, I wouldn't want you to be upset and not let me play again. This really is a fun game. Has it been around long?" She stacked the chips in perfect piles in front of her.

"About thirty years," Fred said, picking up the cards to deal. "You know you'll start the betting this time. You're the blind."

"Okay," she nodded innocently. She knew exactly how long folks had been drawing a chair up to a poker table. Her brothers had taught her well. *Keep a stone face, don't let your emotions rule your bets, there's no such thing as a lucky hand, you'd better do your math, figure the odds, and absolutely do not do anything repetitively that lets them know you are bluffing.*

"Fifty dollars," she tossed chips into the middle of the table before she ever looked at her cards. A dumb move by a stupid woman. It was written all over their faces and it might sure enough cost her a bunch of money, but then it would be money well spent if they thought she truly had just had beginner's luck. Besides, the wind had begun to howl outside and the ship wasn't as steady on its course as it had been. Though slight, she could feel the sway, and the game might not last as long as it could have if the captain sent them all to their rooms.

"You really aren't very smart," Beady said, tossing in his ante.

"I don't suppose so, but isn't it a fun way to spend the

night?" she looked at her cards. Four tens with a king kicker. Let them talk about how dumb she was later when she walked away with all their money. Maybe her brothers had been wrong in teaching her there was no such thing as luck. Maybe her wedding ring had brought her a measure of good fortune. She toyed with it, noticing that Beady and Big-burly both watched her closely. They'd think she was bluffing and that was good.

Bets went around the table. Big-burley tossed out three cards and asked for three replacements. Beady threw away one. The replacement caused an ever so faint twitch at the corners of his mouth. If he had a royal flush she'd be busted. Her oldest brother said to know when to hold 'em and know when to fold 'em. She'd had nothing when she went outside for a breath of air, so she'd hold 'em and hope for the best.

Bets went around again. She'd put everything in the pot except about a hundred dollars. Just enough to play one more game if she failed. Beady looked prouder and prouder of his hand. He could hardly sit still in his anxiety. He fully well intended to show that little snippet of a woman that this was a game for men, not silly women who'd fought with their husbands.

"Got quad sixes with a jack kicker," he laid them out on the table and reached to rake in the pile.

"I do believe quad tens with a king kicker will beat that. Can you imagine both of us getting all four of the cards out of that deck? Only difference is that I drew them from the start and it took several rounds to gather yours up," she said.

"I'm finished," Big-burly said. "I ain't fightin' beginner's luck anymore tonight, lady. You and your husband have another fight, you come on out here, and we'll take back our money from you."

"Me too," Fred stood up. "Who'd have thought that a person could win like that two times in a row? Must be your lucky night, little lady. Want me to help you take the chip tray over to the window and cash it in?"

"I can do it. Which window?" Adelida asked. "You fellers have been real nice to let me sit in on the game. Maybe tomorrow night after the storm is over, we'll play again."

"You bet we will," Beady said grumpily. "You won't win like that two nights in a row."

She was amazed at how much money she had when she cashed in her chips. She carried the money back to her room where Rueben mumbled in his sleep. Removing her dress and camisole, she tucked the bills into a pocket inside her camisole and sewed the top shut with the tiniest stitches.

Tomorrow, she decided, she would tell Rueben and they'd go their separate ways. The wailing wind and another sway in the ship took her to the window to check out the storm brewing outside. She'd never seen such a sight as the wall of clouds approached from the south. It was a full fledged hurricane or she'd give her winnings to Big-burly with a smile on her face. Without wasting a single motion, she redressed herself, patting the place close to her ribs where the bundle of money was tightly sewn. Then she went back to the window to check the cloud formation again.

The wheel on the side of the ship crumpled even as she watched.

"Rueben, wake up. There's a terrible storm out there," she shook him hard enough to rattle his teeth.

He came up from his recurring dream about a wedding. He was the groom, but he couldn't see his wife's face for the thick lace veil. "What?"

"Get dressed. The ship's wheel on this side just went into the drink," she said, tossing him his pants and shirt.

"Settle down, Adelida. It's just a storm. Even if we did lose a wheel, that doesn't mean the storm is going to sink us," Rueben said as he yawned and stretched before buttoning his shirt and getting dressed. Just as he pulled on his boots, the emergency bell sounded and the ship tilted drastically to the side, slinging Adelida right into his arms.

"All passengers prepare to evacuate this ship," a steward bellowed time after time in the dining room.

"Ride it out, huh?" Adelida asked.

"Guess not," Rueben said, his blood running cold at the idea of facing the relentless rain and wind in a lifeboat that was nothing but a tub of wood. He'd rather stay on the ship.

"I've got something to tell you, Rueben."

"It'll have to wait," he said, drawing her close to his side and opening the door. "If we live through this mess, you can tell me later."

Chapter Six

Other than the ship's captain and two remaining officers, Rueben and Adelida were the last ones to leave the ship. Rain fell in sheets, soaking them in seconds after being loaded and dropped into waves as tall as two-story houses. Fierce winds and driving rain swept them away in a confusing vortex. With a moan barely audible above the storm, the ship lost her dignity and sank before they were tossed out into a never-ending sea of gray. Adelida clung to the little life boat with both hands and hoped the pieces of the ship blowing around them, both in the angry waters and spinning through the gusting wind, didn't kill them.

To think they'd survive such a storm in nothing more than a canoe when a ship the size of what they'd been on had been lost, was sheer lunacy. Why had the captain put his passengers in these tiny boats and set them out in the middle of the storm? No one could live through waves so high and winds so fierce. After the way Adelida had suckered Rueben, she certainly wasn't expecting any stray miracles to materialize, either. She thought of the money sewn so carefully in her camisole. Little good it would do her now. The next big wave would probably take them to the bottom of the ocean to a watery grave. She shut her eyes, expecting to see her life flash before her. Wasn't that the final thing a person saw? A brief recounting of all her sins so she could beg forgiveness in the last breath of life? All that appeared behind her eyelids was the sight of Rueben's face when he regained consciousness in the bank. *Lord*, she prayed fervently, *get me through this storm alive and I promise I will tell him the truth.* When she opened her eyes the small boat was teetering on the top of a wave so high it nauseated her, then it tumbled down, down, down and hit another breaker with enough force to rattle her teeth. Her life flashing before her would be a blessing compared to the fear clenching at her insides. She'd never live long enough to own up to all her lies.

The little boat dipped and swayed and several inches of ocean water sprayed inside to fill the bottom. Rueben screamed something about land, but she could only feel the cold fingers of death wrapping around her soul. Her long, black hair whipped in her face, the tendrils snaking around her neck like a hanging rope. Rueben bailed water from around her feet with his cupped hands, but she was a stone statue, unable to tear her hands from the sides of the boat to help him. She saw other lifeboats, some capsizing and the people flailing like rag dolls in the vicious storm. Others seemed to be hanging on in their boats but going away from her. Rueben kept trying to bail water from around her feet, and she kept wondering what the use was. None of the passengers from the ship would ever live to tell the story of the great hurricane.

Rueben could see beyond the relentless rain just enough to know there was land not far away. If only he could keep them afloat and the wind didn't change directions and send them back out to sea, they might have a chance of survival. He remembered seeing a whole string of small uninhabited islands when he traveled to Louisiana the year before. It was another new memory, but he didn't have time to dwell on it. He had to keep them from sinking or they'd be washed out into the ocean and drown. Adelida had to be scared senseless. She hadn't let go of the sides of the boat since the captain had helped her inside it, but that was a good thing because it was probably what balanced things while he kept bailing water with his hands. He was glad she wasn't having a case of the vapors. A scared woman he could contend with. He'd have been tempted to toss a hysterical one to the sharks.

He looked up again and his eyes were not deceiving him. There was land not far away. They were in the shallows, the wind sending them toward it. "Help me!" he screamed in Adelida's ear, trying to make her hear above the tempest.

She tried to get the strands of limp, wet hair out of her face by shaking it so she could hear what he said, but it didn't work. She leaned toward him until her ear was so close to his mouth she could feel the warmth of his breath through the storm. "Help me. Land."

Her dark eyes darted toward where he was pointing. It was there, but they'd have to fight the waves. She let go of the sides of the boat and carefully threw a leg out over the side.

"What in the devil are you doing, woman?" he yelled.

It was a terrible chance, but if they were that close, surely the water wouldn't be over her head. The driving waves were traveling in that direction and she could swim or let them carry her body to shore if it was deeper than she thought. Sure enough, when her foot hit bottom, the water only came up to her arm pits. She gripped the sides of the boat and began fighting the wicked waves as she tugged it toward the beach.

Rueben jumped out and the two of them combated the storm for more than half an hour before they finally drug the boat up on the island and to the base of a gnarled old tree a hundred feet inland.

"Help me turn the boat over," Rueben yelled above the still raging storm.

"Why?" she yelled back, pushing hair from her eyes and out of her face.

"Come on. We'll use it for shelter," Rueben guided her under the capsized boat, then he crawled in beside her, wrapping her in his arms as he lowered it over them like a turtle's shell.

Rainwater dripped in past holes that had been knocked in the small craft when they had dragged it inland, but at least it blocked out part of the storm. Adelida snuggled down inside Rueben's embrace, shut her eyes, shuddered once, and fell into exhausted sleep. When she awoke, she'd tell him. It was a promise, and she'd keep it.

Tomorrow.

Pure exhaustion claimed Rueben. He drew his bride closer to his side, gave a brief prayer of thanks for both of them surviving the gale, and listened to the raging squall still wrecking havoc outside. How could Adelida sleep in such a turmoil?

He awoke with a jerk and thought he'd been buried alive. It looked like the slats of a wooden coffin all around him, however his arm hurt too badly for Rueben to be dead. He rolled his neck to one side to see Adelida curled up next to him, her damp clothing torn and clinging to her full bosom. In that split second as he gazed upon her lovely face, heavy lashes resting upon cheeks that looked as if they'd been formed from angel's wings, his memory returned. Thoughts. Ideas. Past. Present. Future. All jumbled up, trying to take center stage and be recognized. He saw Love's Valley. His sister. His two brothers. His cousin Ellie. He remembered what he was doing in Louisiana and why he was in the bank. He'd knocked Adelida Broussau flat on her back and then fell on top of her . . . twice.

He was not married.

He gasped.

She awoke.

"Is it over?" she asked.

"Oh, yes, Adelida, it's over," he grimaced as he freed his arm from around her and kicked the boat away from them.

She sat up, pulled her shoulders up in a stretch and blinked at the hot sun rudely scorching her eyes. The storm was over and they'd survived. All her bones seemed to be working, even if they were a bit stiff and they had made it through with only minor scratches and bruises.

"I said it's over," Rueben said through clamped teeth.

"Well, I'm not blind," she smarted back at him, her stomach grumbling in hunger. "The sun is bright. The water is still and beautiful again. I can see it's over, Rueben."

"Not the storm. The . . . what is that?" He pointed to what appeared to be a huge watering trough on stilts.

"It's a cistern for catching rain water. Guess someone lived on this island at one time. They'd have had to fix something for drinking water," she said. "Probably the wreckers had a station here and . . . why are you looking at me like that?"

"Why did you lie to me?" Rueben asked bluntly.

"I didn't. Those people that we ate with last night, the ones who sat at our table, talked about the shipwrecks in this area. Remember they said there were several each month and that folks made their living from the wreckage, salvaging what they could and reselling it? That's what I figured the cistern is put there for. Sometimes the wreckage floats up on this island and while they're here, they need fresh water."

"I'm not talking about that cistern," he said. "You're not my wife. I didn't marry you. It was Lewiss' wedding I kept remembering. I just ran into you in front of the bank, Adelida. Why did you lie?"

"Seemed to be the logical thing to do right then. Evidently, you got your memory back during the storm. Well, that's right nice, because now I don't have to go figuring out a way to tell you," she brushed past him, ignoring the wicked, mean looks he shot her way. So he'd remembered? How wonderful. She would have told him that day. She wasn't so stupid as to think she could cheat God, and she had made a vow that if she survived the storm, she would own up to her sins.

"Let's see how big this place is and if there's food or if we're going to need to make some gigs and fish. I don't know about you, Rueben, but I'm starving half to death," she said.

He grabbed her by the shoulders. "I want answers."

She shook loose from his grip and slapped at his hands when they reached for her again. "And people in hell want ice water too. I lied because I needed to get out of New Orleans right then. And you can stop snatching at me. You needed someone to take care of you and get you to the ship. I needed to leave town. It was a good arrangement. Now we're on this island and hopefully we can find some sort of food because I'm hungry."

"Who are you?" his tone demanded, as he followed close behind her.

"I'm Adelida Broussau, just like I told you the day you so rudely knocked me down in front of the bank," she said. "And you are Rueben Hamilton who thought he could be quite the Yankee hero and take on three bank robbers with only one gun. The rest of what I told you is the truth. The only lie was that I'm your wife." She marched toward the cistern, the warm white sugar sand, though still damp, felt good on her bare feet. The sun would dry it all out today. If there had been a fishing shack on the island it would have been located near the cistern and there could be the remnants of something to eat there.

"This isn't over, Miss Broussau. You will give me some answers," Rueben said, his voice still cold with anger. Why did Adelida need to leave New Orleans bad enough to ruin her reputation? She'd posed as his wife and no one would believe they'd slept in separate beds.

Was she truly one of the ladies of the night? No, that wasn't possible. Innocence oozed out of her. Adelida ignored him and wandered around the cistern as if looking for a complete breakfast of bacon and eggs to materialize. He wanted to kick something or throw a fit like a two-year-old, but neither would net him a bit of satisfaction. He'd been fooled into believing she was his wife. He set his mouth in a firm line and drew his eyebrows into a solid dark streak above dark, brooding eyes.

From where he stood, fairly close to the cistern, he could see both sides of the island and one end. It must be longer than it was wide. He squinted down the length of it. Nothing but twisted trees and white beaches. No sign of any other life. No passengers from the ship had been washed up on the island with them. He squinted against the sun, shaded his eyes with his hands, and looked at the trees.

"Mangroves, cypress and oranges," she answered his question about the trees before he even asked it. "It might have been a fishing island at one time. If it was there might be the remnants of an old garden since they went to the trouble to build a cistern, but I can't find one."

"How would you know that?" Rueben asked dryly.

"Grew up on the Bayou Penchant on a bateau," she said. "We had an agreement with the sugar plantation owner that we could have an acre of ground for growing food in exchange for the use of our bateau once a year to help get the crop to the warehouse. Where there's a cistern, there's most usually a reason. But there's no garden here so this must be just a wreckage island. But that really is an orange tree over there and they look fairly ripe. And there's coconuts on the ground, so with lots of fresh rainwater, we'll live. Maybe we'll get some of the wreckage by tomorrow and there'll be something we can use in it. One thing's for sure, we'll gather it up, because when the scavengers get here, I intend to use it to bargain my way off this island."

He was amazed. The woman had just barely survived the biggest hurricane he could imagine. It had taken a huge ship to the bottom of the ocean. Her dress was torn and ragged—beyond repair and her dark hair was streaming down her back in disarray. She was barefoot, he'd confronted her with all her lies, and yet she'd taken all of it in one big stride and was delighted to see a tree with oranges on it. He'd seen men lose their minds in the war with less controversy.

"Are you crazy? We're marooned on an island not a lot bigger than the ship we were on. It might be weeks before anyone finds us if they ever do and you're talking like this is some kind of holiday!" Rueben shouted at her.

She popped her hands onto her hips and glared at him again. "We Broussaus are a friendly lot. Quite hospitable. But when we're hungry we turn into something so mean even the 'gaters run from us, and I'm hungry, Rueben. I'm going to eat an orange, then I'm going to make myself a gig, wade out there in the water, and hope I can catch a fish. You can do your best to find some dry sticks and use your Yankee military ingenuity to build a fire or else we'll eat the fish raw. So I'm not married to you. That should bring you great joy since you don't like southern women. We're stuck on an island, like you say not much bigger than the ship we were on, but we'll live. I am a survivor, Rueben, and that's a fact. The first thing we've got to have is food. I grew up fishing for a living, so I'll gig some fish. After that, we'll build some kind of shelter, and then we'll talk about things that don't even matter at this point, sugar."

The muscles in his jaw pulsated. "Don't call me sugar."

"Sorry about that. It's the Cajun in me. We call everyone sugar and it don't mean a thing. Little children are sugar, but then our worst enemies can also be sugar if we're being sarcastic, which I definitely was."

His dark eyes were slits in a face full of fury. His nostrils flared. How dare that snippet of a woman talk to him like that! As if he were a child who couldn't think past the end of his nose. So his job was to start a fire with nothing more than sticks and lots of soaking wet wood. He kicked the sand with his bare foot and wondered just when he'd lost his boots.

What he wouldn't give for a nice, dry tender box and a few matches couldn't be measured in gold or silver. He'd show that silly Cajun a fire. He'd set the whole island on fire and boil half the ocean with the heat. He watched

Adelida tear a stick from one of the gnarled trees populating the island. She shed her skirt on the beach and waded out into the still blue water.

A smile twitched at the corners of his mouth at the sight of her concentrating on the water, searching for a fish that would stay still long enough for her to spear it with a semi-sharp stick. She might have caught fish in the bayou, but he'd be willing to wager that it wasn't with a stick.

He squinted against the sun and stared at the cistern. There was no doubt that someone did indeed build it for fresh water, but how did they plan to get the water out of it? There was no ladder on the side to climb up to the top and fetch it, and no plug underneath and nothing to catch it in. He continued to gaze at the thing. How had it withstood the recent gale? It must be built on pilings of some kind to stand upright after the winds he'd just been through. He checked all six legs. A thin reed-like pipe that resembled bamboo ran from the cistern down the inside of the stilt-like leg and into the sand. He dropped down onto his knees and began to dig, slinging sand off to the side as he followed the line a foot, then two feet. A slight incline made him dig deeper and deeper, the sand giving readily until he hit a rock.

Adelida waded out a little farther. Surely the storm sent a few fish closer to the shores. Just one nice, big one for their dinner would be nice. She'd have to wait until she could build a fire before they could eat because that stupid Rueben was digging in the sand like some kind of puppy hunting for a bone. All she'd asked him to do was prepare a fire. It wasn't like she'd told him he had to hunt down a bear or a deer with his bare hands. She was willing to use the skills she'd learned as a child and gig a fish.

She hoped she could remember how to flint off a flame with a couple of rocks because even if she was hungry, she sure didn't plan on eating the fish raw. And all that crazy man wanted to do was dig a ditch with his bare hands. Maybe the storm had shoved him over the edge of sanity.

"First one without a brain to remember and then one without a brain, period. Just my luck," she said, as she kept one eye on the water and one on Rueben.

He threw himself down beside the trench he'd dug, uncovering the line. Why did the water end there? *Because, stupid, there's something underground where the water is going*, his mind told him bluntly. He jumped up and began dusting away the sand at the top of the rock, working his way to the right until he found wood.

"Aha," he murmured, quickly brushing six inches of sand from a slanted wooden door with rusty hinges on one side and a leather strap for a handle on the other. If the scavengers had a hole to store their horde, then they would most likely keep a tender box down there with matches in it. Just let Adelida come carrying in a fish now. He'd show her he could build a fire big enough to roast a whale.

He tugged at the door until it reluctantly opened with a loud moan not totally unlike the sound the ship had made when it had sunk. He carefully stepped on the first stone step leading down into an enormous cellar. Sunlight fell across a table with a thick candle and a tender box. He lit the candle and turned slowly, expecting to find a guard sleeping out the storm. But there was no guard, only a bunk bed in one corner that hadn't seen a body in many years, if the dust on the covers was an indication. Sure enough, the water line came in through the rocks and ended right above a wash basin located on the top of a table. A cork stuck in the end served as a spigot. Holding the light in his hand, he turned slowly. What he saw took his breath away.

"Rueben, are you all right?" Adelida screams floated down the entrance to the cellar. She'd been concentrating on finding a fish and had stopped keeping an eye on Rueben when suddenly the sand swallowed him. She was certain he'd dug his way into a quick sand pit. She threw her gig on the sandbar and ran all out toward the place she'd seen him last. She didn't want to be married to him, but she also didn't want to spend weeks, months, or maybe even years on a deserted island all alone with no one to talk to either.

"Down here," he called out.

"Where?" She still couldn't see anything and her heart was about to leap right out of her chest.

"Here," his head popped up and he was holding a fat candle, lit with fire.

Now how did he do that? she wondered, stopping dead in her tracks, her cotton drawers dripping water as her eyes widened in surprise.

"We didn't land on a scavenger's island, Adelida. We've been tossed out on a pirate's island. Come and take a look at this," he motioned her down the steps.

"Sweet mercy," she stammered, as he shined the light around the cellar. "They'll kill us for sure when they come back after this."

"I don't think they're coming back, Adelida. Look at the dust on it. These are some kind of foreign coins," he fingered the gold in one of the three trunks laden with old money. "If they were going to return they'd have already come by now."

"What do we do with it?" She asked, squinting at the other three trunks loaded with jewels. Diamonds, rubies, necklaces so fancy they took her breath away. Six trunks worth enough to buy a whole country.

"Well, it's a cinch we can't walk on water and carry it all home to Love's Valley, now isn't it?" he said testily.

"And we sure can't eat it, so we're back to fishing," she said.

"Priceless," he mumbled. "And worthless at the same time."

"Well, we've got fire," she nodded toward the candle, tearing her eyes away from a chest of fancy jewelry. "So guard it carefully and let's get back to the job of catching a fish before we end up being nothing more than a pile of dead bones in here with all this treasure."

"We'll have a place to sleep," he said, motioning toward the bunk bed. "After we eat, maybe we ought to air out those blankets."

She picked up a blanket and it crumbled in her hands. "Rueben, these things have been here for a hundred years. Look," she pulled back sheets and they ripped into shreds. "Have we stumbled upon Blackbeard's cache?"

"Who knows? His or some other pirate who must've stashed his horde then got killed before he came back to claim it. Maybe there really was a Gasparilla and we've stumbled upon the stash he hid in the islands off the tip of Florida. If that's the case, these things were put here more than sixty years ago," Rueben said.

"Is it ours, then?" she asked.

"I suppose it could be. Since possession is the majority of the law. But I don't think we can get it off this island in a life boat, do you? And if we are found by scavengers, you can bet they'd kill us for all this," he said, pushing open a door toward the back of the cellar.

"I think I've found the men they left behind to keep guard," he said. "You better not come in here."

He said it too late. She was already behind him, her dark eyes widening at the sight of two skeletons stretched out on the floor.

"What happened, do you think?" she whispered.

"They most likely got sick with a fever or some such thing and came in here to drink the rest of the wine left behind before they died," he motioned toward the single barrel marked wine on the outside and several others, all empty and lying on their sides.

"A whole cask of wine when we need potatoes or onions or even carrots," she muttered with a shudder. "Shut the door, Rueben, and let's forget what's behind it."

He pulled the door shut. Poor men. They'd waited for their comrades to come back, only to die surrounded by a king's ransom that wouldn't give them passage off the island or medicine to cure their ailment.

He tried to shake off the feeling of doom that told him he and Adelida could very well be the next two people to die on the island.

"I have fire. I've done the job you told me to do. Now you've got to go do yours. Get on out of here and catch a fish, Adelida," he said.

"This isn't funny," she declared.

"No, it's not. Too bad we can't use gold or diamonds for fish bait," he smarted back at her.

"If you don't shut up, I may strangle you and use you for fish bait," she started back up the steps, picking up a jewel-encrusted dagger from the table where the water-line ended. "At least I can make a decent gig with this. It ought to sharpen up a stick real good."

"Make two and I'll help you." He set the candle on the table where he found it, careful that the flame still burned bright. "Right after we both find enough wood to start a fire. There's only a couple of matches left in that tender box, so we'll have to keep the fire going all the time."

"Rain?" she asked.

"We'll build a protected fire if it rains. A small one so we don't lose the flame," he planned ahead. Things didn't look quite so bleak anymore. Surely they hadn't blown so far off the beaten path that the scavengers couldn't find them.

Oh, sure, his conscience chided, *they haven't found that horde down in the cellar. What makes you think they'll find you and Adelida?*

"Then let's go use this worthless, lovely dagger to make us some gigs. I'm glad it's weathered the test of time," she tested it for sharpness and found a fine, honed edge.

He stepped aside to let her go up the stairs first. She wore wet, tattered under garments, a ragged shirtwaist and was carrying a dagger worth more money than what his grandfather paid for Love's Valley. A visual oxymoron if he'd ever seen one. A natural beauty that surpassed all the priceless jewels and sold in the trunks.

Adelida would have been embarrassed by her attire if she'd had an ounce of dignity left in her. But the storm and near-death experience had robbed her of every drop of self-respect, and besides, she was hungry. Too bad she couldn't roast diamonds and eat them. Maybe the scavengers would be out hunting for treasures before long and she could use the money still sewn in her camisole to buy the two of them passage to the next port. Rueben was going to have to pretend to be her husband and he wasn't going to like that one bit, but he had no other choice. If she wasn't married, then the scavengers might shoot Rueben and do unspeakable things to her. However, if they were a married couple, she'd have a much better chance of survival. Rueben Hamilton could pretend. And he'd better do a good job of it too, or she'd shoot him herself.

Chapter Seven

"Guess we'll have to learn how far away to lay the fish if we want it done on the inside and not burned on the outside," she said.

"Guess so. Hey, what's that?" Rueben pointed toward something bobbing in the water, the waves bringing it closer and closer to shore.

"A wine cask. A trunk. I don't know. Let's go see." She raced to the edge of the beach and right out into the water.

They pulled the trunk to shore and pried the lock off the swollen wood. It contained the sodden clothing of a woman two sizes larger than Adelida and a man at least twenty pounds bigger and four inches shorter than Rueben. They hung the clothing from the branches of a mangrove tree to dry. She'd no more than gotten the three dresses, two pairs of trousers and two shirts, along with a change of undergarments for a lady and one for a man, arranged as best she could when Rueben called to her from the banks of the shore where he was pulling in lengths of wood. She ambled down to the shore, taking her time beneath the unrelenting, blazing sun. She would

74

have gladly shed her undergarments and camisole and swam in the cool ocean waters if Rueben hadn't been there. But he was, and they weren't married, and she hadn't lost every single ounce of her modesty yet.

Pulling in boards and laying them out to dry like fish fillets on the warm sand was hard work, but neither of them stopped.

"We could do this with fish if we have to stay here long. Lay it out on wood slats to dry. We could even dry orange slices. Reckon this came from the ship? What are we going to do with it? The scavengers aren't going to be interested in old wood from the sides of a ship," Adelida said.

"No, they aren't, but it'll come in handy to build a shanty. We'll use the cistern for the roof and build it around those six legs it stands on. Don't you sunburn?" Rueben asked.

"I'm Cajun, Rueben. We don't burn, we just get darker and darker. Why are we going to trouble ourselves with the building of a shanty when there's a cellar we can stay in?"

"When the scavengers get here, if they do, you want to take them down in that cellar and show them where we been sleeping?" He shaded his eyes and scanned the gentle waves for anything else that might wash up.

"You're right," she nodded, hating to give him even that much credit. "Guess we'd better build us a shack. Besides, I'm not so sure I could sleep down in that hole with those two skeletons in the next room," she added. "Without nails how do you plan to do a job like that?"

"We'll use what we can find on the island," he said.

She snorted.

"Oh ye of little faith," he intoned dramatically. However, if he was honest he'd have to admit that he, himself, had little faith of them ever being rescued. Stranded on an island with a shrewish woman who could barely tolerate his presence surely wasn't what he would have wished for when he and his brothers played the childish game of "What would you do if you were on an island with . . ."

"Don't you be doubting my faith," she picked up a length of wet wood and began dragging it toward the cistern. She gazed out into the water. Nothing but an occasional piece of wood bobbing up and down. No more trunks. They really must have been thrown a long way from where the ship went down. The lumber and trunk might have even come from another ship. After all, *The Queen* hadn't been the only ship in the water when the hurricane turned everything topsy-turvy.

"Do you think anyone else might wash up on the island, like we did?" she asked.

"Could be, but I doubt it. I rather think they'd have been here by now. This area is full of tiny islands. Most likely there are other survivors scattered all over them," he said.

When the sun was nothing more than an sliver setting out where the blue water kissed the brilliant orange sky, they stopped working and threw themselves down a distance from the fire Rueben had kept going all afternoon. Heat was something they could do without. They were dirty, tired, and irritable, but they'd managed to use lengths of green vines to lash the pieces of wood to the legs of the cistern and had walls two feet all the way around it. Rueben had removed the cork from the water line down into the cellar. Using the dagger, he cut the supply line off a foot from ground level and quickly stuck the cork back into the new place. He broke the remaining several inches of line off below ground level and refilled the entire trench with sand. Now there was no sign at all that the water had ever been channeled into the cellar, and he fervently hoped it was hidden so well that the scavengers, if and when they arrived, wouldn't see that the line had been recently cut.

"So now we've got a fancy new home complete with running water," Adelida said. "But supper isn't ready, is it? So do we dine on coconuts and oranges or do we fish?"

"I'm too tired to fish," Rueben said.

"Then I guess it's oranges. We'll bank the fire and go to bed early in the beginnings of our cistern mansion. Tomorrow morning we'll have a fine breakfast, trust me. I'll take care of those clothes and get them packed back in the trunk before I turn in." She slipped one of the dresses over her head, roping it in at the waist with a sash. The wide, sweeping skirts slowed her down as she walked through the sand.

"This ain't goin' to work," she declared.

"Oh, yes it will. See here how the vines hold the pieces of wood to the legs," Rueben shot her a mean look. How dare she decide after they'd worked for hours and hours that his idea wouldn't work.

"I'm not talking about your carpentry skills," she unbuckled the belt and stepped out of the dress, draping it over one of the two foot walls. "I'm talking about this dress. It wasn't made for wading through sand. I'll just save it until we're rescued. Talkin' of which, soon as we spot a ship, we'll have to work fast and cover up that door to the cellar." Wearing nothing but her drawers and camisole, she stretched out beside Rueben, keeping at least three feet between them.

"I'd thought of that already. It's back behind the trees a

bit so we'll have a little cover. When we spot the ship, you should sit on the trunk right out in the open and they'll see you. That'll bring them to shore and give me time to cover the door," he said.

"Oh sure, use me for bait," she said.

"What are you doing? I thought we were going to bed early," he asked, watching her every movement. She moved like a lazy cat, one who didn't have a care in the world, but that was just a disguise. Adelida could move in for the kill. He'd watched her spear that big fish, watched her grab a piece of wood just out of her reach. She could be a dangerous woman, and he'd do well to keep a watchful eye on her. Sassy. Dangerous. What other qualities did she possess?

"We are. I'm just taking time to put this dress away. Hey, what's this?" she asked herself, pulling at a corner in the chest and bringing up the top of a false bottom. She giggled when she found a sapphire necklace and several other pieces of fine jewelry in the bottom of the trunk. "Just what we need, more jewels," she held up the necklace, the dark jewels almost black with nothing but the light of a full moon to illuminate them.

"No potatoes or onions?" he asked.

"Just more jewelry and a stack of money. Looks to be more than a thousand dollars. Shall we use it for kindling?"

"Put it all back, and hopefully we can get out of here with it intact. That would be enough to take us all the way home," he said.

"Us?"

He stopped short. She wasn't going home with him. They weren't married. He'd forgotten in their easy camaraderie. And so soon after he'd just given himself a lecture on the necessity of being aware of her charms.

"Each of us. Wherever we want to go," he blushed, hoping she thought his red face was the result of too much sun.

"You still going home to those mountains?" she asked.

"If we get off here in one piece I suppose I am," he answered. "And you? You going back to your bayou? Why didn't you go there to begin with?"

"Because I didn't have any money," she said honestly, returning to her sand bed and lacing her own hands behind her head just like Rueben. "Victor LaSalle saw to that."

"Victor LaSalle? What did you have to do with that trash?" Rueben asked.

"Well, that's one thing we can agree on. Victor is trash," she told him. "He married my sister Maria and brought her to New Orleans from the bayou. When the war started, he smelled fortune and found it during the war. My sister was shot in a freak accident and Victor told me I had to get out of town or I'd be the next one to die. Then he went to the bank and cleaned out the account my sister and I had there—money that I'd made when I sold my papa's bateau. So there I was with no money to leave and the threat of death hanging above me. You ran into me at the front of the bank just before I found out I didn't have a penny to my name," she yawned and covered her mouth with a hand.

"So when we get rescued and get to a port, are you going back to the bayou?" he asked, almost adding, "where you belong" before he bit his tongue.

"No, my family is all dead. Mama when I was a girl, my three brothers in the war. Papa a little more than a month ago. Maria by a bullet that I'll never be fully convinced Victor didn't shoot. I want to see your mountains before I decide what I'm going to do. When I was a little girl I saw a book with pictures of mountains and a pretty little stream, and in the background there were flowers by a house that had a foundation. I want to see that sight with my own eyes. It's haunted me ever since I saw it in that book."

"Love's Valley," he nodded, without looking at her. She'd just described his valley, but he was not taking her home with him. Heaven help him if he came dragging Adelida in. His sister Indigo would go up in flames halfway to heaven. She'd already been moaning and groaning in her letters about Monroe marrying that Texan and their cousin, Ellie, marrying the Texan's brother. He frowned in the darkness. Not that he'd want to marry Adelida anyway.

"Is that what your valley looks like?" she asked.

"Yes, it is," he answered. "Little valley between two mountain ranges. My family owns the whole thing. Older brother, Monroe, met a woman from Texas and married her last fall. Her brother stayed on in the valley to help find my cousin who'd been abducted. Winter set in before he could get out and go back to Texas and they wound up together. So there's new homes being built in the valley. But, wait a minute, you told me all of this when we were on the ship. How did you know?"

"I read your letters," she said.

"You did what? You read my personal mail?" He clenched his teeth.

"Of course. I unpacked your clothes and read the letters. How else could I know you or where to take you if I didn't read them? Don't get all huffy. If you'd had letters from a wife, I would have put you in the care of your friend, John Jacobs, and disappeared," she said.

"But that's rude," he said.

"Yes, it is, but it was necessary. You might as well forgive me and forget it. We're the only ones on this island and being angry with each other isn't very smart."

"I want to see Love's Valley," she changed the subject. "Just look at it and then I'll go on to the next big town and find myself a place. Surely that sapphire necklace is worth enough to get me a start. That and what I intend to take out of that cellar and put in the false bottom of our chest."

"So we agree on that much. I thought I'd take some of the coins."

"I'll give you half the space. Good night, Rueben. We wake really early for breakfast," she said, her voice trailing off as her eyes fluttered.

"Good night Adelida," he murmured. Breakfast would be another coconut busted open with the point of the dagger and it didn't matter what time he awoke for that. When they were rescued, Adelida Broussau might see his mountains, if she had a desire to do so. She could ride in a fancy stagecoach or hire a private rig and chaperone to take her there. But, as much as he admired her, he wouldn't be escorting her on her voyage.

Not a fat chance.

None whatsoever.

"Wake up, Rueben," Adelida shook his shoulder. "It's time to gather up breakfast."

He barely opened his left eye, just enough to see that the moon still hung by a thread of sparkling stars. There was no way it was morning. He'd barely gone to sleep. What kind of game was this crazy Cajun woman playing?

"Open your eyes. We're going clam digging," she giggled, pulling at his hand.

"I'm sleeping until the sun is straight up," he rolled over on his side and propped his head on a crooked arm.

"You are getting up right now or I'll eat clams right in front of you. I won't share one bite, and that's a fact. You can sleep this afternoon when it's too hot to work," she slapped him on the back.

"Then eat in front of me," he mumbled. "I don't care. I'll starve before I get up in the middle of the night."

"Your choice, sugar," she said sweetly.

"Don't call me that! I told you not to call me that," he sat up, wide awake and ready to do battle.

"Well, the sleeping tiger awakes, huh?" she taunted as she grabbed up the gigs and ran toward the water's edge.

"Drat that woman. May we be rescued today and I never have to see her again," he picked up a handful of sand and slung it. Clam digging in the middle of the night. What else could she think of to rile him? *Plenty,* his conscience said loudly. *Remember, if you let her anger you, then she has power over you. Remember what you were taught in the military. If you let the enemy anger you, he rules. Keep your rage out of the battle. Fight with a cool head.*

Rueben was beginning to understand more fully the benefits of bachelorhood. Maybe he'd be the son who lived in the old home place and took care of his mother until she died. He'd keep company with several women, going to dinner or to a church picnic, but never getting serious about any of them. He could enjoy his nieces and nephews and leave his amassed fortune to them.

"Clam digging," he said. "And I suppose she's got all the ingredients for a nice pot of clam chowder hiding in those skimpy undergarments." He threw himself back in the sand and imagined a nice, big, fluffy feather mattress covered with crisp, ironed sheets, a cool mountain breeze blowing out the sheer curtains on the windows, and the aroma of bacon floating up the stairs from the kitchen. His stomach growled and he sat back up. She was busy with a stick grubbing in the sand, tossing something that looked vaguely like a rock into the pan she'd brought up from the cellar. The plink of each clam hitting the metal pan was enough to keep him from going back to sleep.

"So you decided to join in the fun, sugar?" She looked up and saw him standing in front of her.

"If you call me that again, I'm going to the other side of the island and never speaking to you again," he picked up a sharp stick and stuck it in the sand. What could be so hard about digging up clams? Was he hungry enough to eat them raw, because she sure didn't have a pot of boiling water, much less milk and potatoes to make them palatable.

"Oh, are we getting a divorce? Splitting the blanket? All because of one little endearment?" She reached down into the hole she'd made with the stick and pulled out a clam that had to be at least six inches across.

"We weren't married and when we were, you didn't call me sugar," he fished around in the pool of water filling the hole he'd dug with his stick. Nothing.

"When we were married I didn't want to do or say anything that might encourage you," she said, squinting until she found just the right spot to dig again.

"Now that we're not married, you can encourage me?" he asked, wondering why she'd been so successful at finding the clams. Maybe it was because she looked like she'd been rolled in wet sand all the way to her arm pits.

"No, now that we're not married, I can be who I really am—Adelida Broussau, who says what she wants and calls everyone sugar, just like all the other bayou women.

Would you rather I call you *cher*?" She pulled up another giant clam and tossed it into the pan.

"I'd rather you didn't call me anything but Rueben," he said.

"*Bon Dieu*, you are a testy one when you don't get enough sleep. Ain't never dug clams before, have you *mon ami*?" She giggled.

"And what does all that mean?"

"*Bon Dieu*? Something my mama would have washed my mouth out with soap for using. It means 'good God.' *Mon ami*? Well, it doesn't mean I love you. It means, 'my friend.' I suppose we can be friends since we're stuck on this island until mid-day together."

Friends? That was a whole new outlook. He'd been married to her for nearly a week, or so he thought. Just looking at all that long, black hair made his hands itch to touch it again like he did the night he brushed it for her. A glance at those full, sensuous lips and the remembrance of the effect they had on his heart when he thought he was married to Adelida drew him up short. He'd loved her in his short memory like a man loved a real wife. Then he'd come close to hating her when he'd figured out she'd lied. And now she'd called him her friend? Could they be that? No, he didn't think so. Not with a bayou Cajun.

"Mid-day? What makes you think we'll be rescued so quickly?"

"You've got to learn to find clams first. Stand with your back to the ocean. See that little dimple in the sand? That means there's a clam down there. Stick your gig in at an angle like so," she showed him the process. "Now dig a hole and go fishing with your fingers. Carefully, though. The edges are sharp and you can bring back a bloody finger if you're careless. Which reminds me, we need to take those stitches out of your head today. We'll do that while breakfast is cooking. Now, about mid-day. The ship will arrive when the sun is high in the sky, and we'll be rescued."

"Oh, and what makes you so sure?" He did like she said and, sure enough, found a nice big clam hiding below the dimple in the sand.

"Ah, that would be a quahog for sure," she said, tossing in one of her own right behind his catch.

"A what?" he asked, finding another tiny hold in the sand.

"A quahog. They're the biggest. Somewhere around six inches across them. The razor clams are about four to five inches. Butter clams are about two to three inches. And the little neck ones are an inch and a half or so. The little ones make the best chowder. Tender, mild tasting," she said, working the whole time and rapidly filling the pan.

"Thank you for the lesson on clams," he said dryly. "Now what makes you think we'll see a ship at mid-day?"

"Have you ever heard of Marie Laveaux?" she asked, poking her gig into another hole in the sand.

"Of course. You don't live long in New Orleans without that name coming up. She's the voodoo queen of the whole South, isn't she? What's that got to do with a ship at mid-day?"

"That she is," Adelida giggled. "She read my palms. My sister took me there. She said I was in for a big adventure and someday my dreams would all come true. Well, today my dream is that a ship will come and rescue me. You'd better make a wish for the same thing because I've got a feeling we could end up killing each other if we have to stay on this island very long."

"I'm wishing and wishing," he said seriously. "But what makes you think the rescue ship will take on passengers? We sure can't show them any jewels or those gold coins," he said.

"I've got money from a poker game. I sewed it into my camisole, and there's the money in the trunk. Lots of it. Even if they charge us ten times the going rate, we've got money to spare," she said. "Don't look at me like that, *mon ami*."

"You did what?" he stood straight up and shouted. "No wife of mine plays poker!"

"I suppose not. But since I was not your wife and will never be your wife, I played poker and won the money. I was going to tell you the truth the next morning. Now I have the money and it will get us off this island. However, you will have to be my husband. My virtue could be in danger," she said. "We have enough clams now for a good bake. The fire is ready. I'll just have to gather some seaweed. Take the pan on up to the fire, and we'll at least have full bellies when our ship comes in."

"Sure," he mumbled as he carried the pan back to the waning fire. She could have her little fantasies. "And if wishes were carrots and potatoes, we could make a pot of soup."

She ignored his mumbling and dug up two armloads of seaweeds, dropped them into the bottom of a shallow pit where a fire had heated hot rocks. She dumped the clams in with the seaweed, ran quickly back to the edge of the water, and brought another armload, which she used to cover the clams. "Now we wait a while until they're steamed. I need a clam shucking knife, but the dagger will have to do. We can bring the trunk down to the shore while we're waiting and cover up the cellar door with sand. That way we'll be ready."

"Adelida, no ship is coming today. It's only been two days since the wreck. They wouldn't even know there was a wreck until yesterday when we didn't arrive at the next port of call."

"We'll be ready. If it doesn't come today then it might come tomorrow. If not then, the next day. We will just be sure to be ready. Because my dreams will come true," she looked him right in the eyes without blinking.

Chapter Eight

His stomach full, Rueben laid back and watched a gorgeous sunrise. The red-orange ball just peeping over the edge of the far, watery horizon sent out long, feathery rays slicing through the puffy cloud-like pale peach colored gauze drifting over white cotton balls. Dolphins arched up out of the water, dark silhouettes against a brilliant sun. Simple perfection, or so he thought, until a mosquito the size of a buzzard lit on the top of his foot and attempted to suck every drop of blood from his body. He swatted at the bug, leaving a splotch of red on his hand and foot alike.

"Draw nearer to the fire," Adelida said. "I'll throw in some coconut husks. Mosquitoes hate them."

"How do you know so much?" Rueben asked.

"I grew up in the bayou. It's not so very different from this. Well, it is but it isn't. Water is water, though. It begets mosquitoes as well as fish," she said, shutting her eyes against the bright daylight. "We didn't have dolphins playing, though. Only 'gaters and swamp rats as big as house cats. We never saw anything like this. Mainly trees, both living and stumps. Sunrise meant the darkness lightened somewhat."

"Do you miss it?" he asked.

"Sure, I do. It was home for my whole life 'cept for the last month. But you know what I liked the most? When Papa would bring the bateau to shore to work the garden plot or to gather in water and supplies. I liked having my feet on solid ground," she said.

"What is the bayou like?" he asked, flopping over on one side to look at her.

"It's a world of its own. The sounds of the 'gaters growling, the chirping of the tree frogs and the hoots of the owls, makes for its own orchestra out there. It's eerie at night with the moss dripping from the cypress trees, and the moonlight, when there's a moon, casts mysterious shadows. The smell is rich. Jasmine, azalea, verbena, wisteria all mixed up with what is just plain old swamp water. One minute your nose says, 'ah, what glorious aromas,' the next minute it's snarling up with the odor of those same flowers dropping their dying blossoms in the water to rot," she said. "What about your mountains? What do they smell like?"

"I'm not sure the mountains smell like anything," he chuckled. "They feel like more than smell like. This time of year it's summer and everything is green. Not nearly as hot and humid as the weather in Louisiana. Nice, cool evenings and mornings with dew on the grass. Fall is nippy and everything turns orange and burgundy. Spring is mint green and we all get the itch to plant something. Winter is snow."

"Snow," she said, reverently. "I can't imagine something so beautiful."

"Never seen snow?"

"Not one time. Seen a lot of floods and storms, but not

snow," she squirmed under the close scrutiny of his gaze. "Now, what are we going to do all morning?"

"Work on our shelter," he sat up. "Then about noon time we'll see if you can gig another one of those big fish for our lunch. If I fillet it, could you cook it with the seaweed like you did the clams?"

"Sure," she agreed. "But have some faith. The ship will come and we won't need the shelter."

"I'd feel a little safer if we had the whole thing enclosed. The scavengers might take weeks to arrive if they ever do," he scanned the beach area for more wood.

"Oh, ye of little faith," she intoned in a deep voice like his. "But I will help you to keep from dying of instant boredom. What is that?"

He followed her pointing finger, half-expecting to see the wheels of a ship in the distance. They shaded their eyes with their hands and watched the waves bring the big item closer and closer. Finally, as if on cue, they arose at the same time and waded out into the warm water to bring their catch to shore. It was an armoire, doors closed tight and locked, bobbing along as if it weighted no more than a palm leaf. Working together, they guided it to the beach, but that's where the job ended. They couldn't move the huge piece of furniture any further.

"The tide will take it away from us tonight," she huffed, out of breath.

"We'll be on the ship by then. Remember?"

"Not if your doubts keep it from arriving today," she said, her own belief in the dream fading as the light of day brightened everything around her. "What if we put it on runners? The sand is what's slowing us down."

"The sand and the fact the thing weighs more than the anchor of the ship it came out of," Rueben said, throwing himself down on the beach and staring at the thing. The wood had swollen and would no doubt split when the sun dried it. No scavengers would be interested in the whole thing. Maybe the doors could be salvaged. He picked up the dagger, lying beside the pan full of clam shells, and pried at the lock.

"You'll ruin it," she yelled at him. "Don't. I can pick the lock with a hairpin."

"Adelida, it doesn't matter whether the lock is broken or not. What's inside is what the wreckers will be interested in, not the armoire itself. It's probably filled with more clothes anyway," he said.

"I don't care. Don't smash it," she squatted beside him and in a few minutes had the lock opened with a hairpin. Sure enough, there were clothes. Dresses for a matronly lady. Deep blue and purple satin with lace trim, big enough that two women Adelida's size could have crawled inside them and still had room. There was no men's clothing though, so unless something else washed ashore, Rueben was going to have to be content to be rescued in trousers four inches above his ankle. She pulled open one of the three drawers at the bottom of the dress rack.

"Look here, sugar," she grinned. "No potatoes or onions, but here's someone's silver. Why would anyone carry their silver flatware with them on a trip? The ship provides spoons and knives, so why carry your own?"

"I told you not to call me sugar," he drew his dark eyebrows down in a glare.

"Well, excuse me," she retorted.

"Maybe the old woman was going to a granddaughter's wedding and was taking the silver to her for a gift," he said.

"What makes her old?" Adelida argued.

"Look at the size of these dresses," he pulled one up

and held it to his own frame. "She was nearly as tall as me and was twice as wide."

"Purple is not your color and being tall doesn't make a woman old," Adelida said, jerking the wet dress from him and carrying it to the same tree branches she'd used to dry clothing the day before. At this rate, they'd be well-dressed if not well-fitted. Well-dressed and starving for good food. All the edible things from the kitchen of the sunken ship must be sitting in the bottom of the ocean providing food for all the fish.

"The silver, now, that's something the wreckers would be interested in. That much alone should get us off the island," he said, pulling open another drawer to find a velvet pouch filled with money.

"How much is there?" She was so close to his shoulder that the warmth of her breath kissed his neck, causing shivers to chase up his backbone.

"Looks to be a thousand or so," he said. "It's wet. We need to take it up to the shelter and spread it out to dry."

"It'll dry faster right here," she picked up the pan of clam shells. "We'll use these to hold it down. The sun will take care of it in no time."

"If we can keep the wreckers from knowing about all this money, we'll be able to get all the way to . . ." he paused.

"I'll sew it inside my underwear like I did the poker money," she said. "Oh, don't look at me that way. I'll share it with you, all but my poker money, that is. That's mine. I won it fair and square, but the rest I'll share when we go our separate ways."

A stinging pang hit his heart. He was quick to dismiss it, though and glad that she wasn't still entertaining notions of going with him to Love's Valley. He began to help her separate the bills and lay them out in the sand to dry.

"Maybe enough money will wash up that when you sew

it all in your undergarments you can fill up one of these dresses," he nodded toward the armoire.

She slapped at his arm, amazed that there was a sinking feeling in her insides at just the touch of her hand on his bare skin. "But that does give me an idea. Wonder if there's a sewing kit anywhere in that thing."

"What are you going to sew? A tent? We could use all the material in those dresses to finish siding up our shelter," he said, counting as he laid out the bills in a uniform line. "Five hundred dollars. That should get us somewhere."

"Should. Is that equal to what you lost in the storm?" she asked, digging around in the next drawer and shouting with glee when she found a small sewing kit. There were two needles, two wooden spools of thread, one in black and one white, and a thimble that was big on her thumb, but a little pad of soft fabric could make it fit her middle finger. There was also a pair of miniature scissors with the shape of a goose neck on the handle.

"I left Louisiana with three thousand dollars in my pocket, so when we share what we've got, I'm still a little short. But hey, I don't have a wife, so that'll make up the difference. So, do we make a tent?" He smiled at the excitement in her eyes. "Or is that sewing stuff going to grow you some potatoes and onions?"

"No, but it's going to buy me all the potatoes and rice I can eat for a lifetime," she said. "I'm going to make a thief's garment out of one of those dresses. I hope you're right about the ship not coming today, because I don't know if I'll have time if it does."

"A thief's garment?" Rueben asked, the smile fading quickly. Just exactly who was this woman?

"Sure, remember the book I told you about? The one with the picture of the mountains and the house with a foundation? The story was about a thief who stole things to put in his house but it didn't make him happy. It told about his garment. A cloak that held pockets on the inside. I'm going to size down one of those dresses and use the excess to put pockets on the inside of the under-skirt to hold more of what is in the cellar."

"You don't have to," Rueben said. "I'm going to ask the ship's captain what the longitude and latitude for this island is, kind of in conversation so we'll know how far we blew off course. My family is into a lot of different business ventures. When we dock in Savannah, I'll tell my brother Reed about this and he'll take care of it from there. A ship will come and take everything that's here back to Hamilton Enterprises."

"And just when were you going to tell me about this, Mr. Rich Man?" She popped her hands on her hips and glared at him.

"When it was done, I'd planned on sending you half of the proceeds. It would be enough to buy you more than one valley in the mountains. You can have a mansion on a foundation. Every suitor on the whole eastern coast of the United States will be after your hand," he said, not look-ing at her.

"Sure you were," she said.

"Adelida, I really was. I promise. I wanted it to be a surprise. You'd have plenty to keep you secure with what's in the bottom of the trunk, but if my company takes possession of all that's down there, you can see the world. You can live in Europe. You can travel anywhere you want," Rueben told her. "Trust me."

Sure, she'd trust a Yankee. About as far as she could pick the good-looking man up and throw him. "I don't think so. I think I'll just stay right by your side until I see the reports on what your company finds. I think you and I are going to be traveling partners all the way to your Love's Valley. I will stay in a nearby hotel until the treasure is tallied up and my half is delivered safely to a bank or several banks."

"You're not going to Love's Valley with me," he declared, the words spat from clenched teeth.

"Oh, but I am," she said. "Until my half of that king's ransom is in my hands I'm sticking to my dear husband like glue."

"I'm not your husband," he said.

"Tell it to those people," she pointed to the faintest outline of a ship on the far horizon. "I figure they'll be sending a lifeboat to rescue us when they see our fire. I reckon we'd better build it up a little higher so they can see the smoke for sure, and then we'd best get our misfitted clothes on our bodies, right after we drag our trunk down here. I'm not leaving without it, Rueben."

An icy knot of something unexplainable and intangible filled his soul. Adelida Broussau in Shirleysburg. *Bon Dieu*, as she'd said.

The sun was high in the sky when two lifeboats were lowered from the ship's side down into the water and began to move slowly toward the seashore. Each boat carried one man with two oars that dipped rhythmically in and out of the water.

The silver flatware laid on the clothing inside the open trunk. Rueben hoped they had enough to buy them passage to the nearest port on the wrecker. Adelida hoped Rueben didn't decide to sell her out to the wreckers so he could keep the whole treasure for himself.

The two little boats made close to shore and then one of the men shouted. "Hello, are you the only two here?"

Adelida wasn't sure what wreckers were supposed to look like, but somehow she didn't think they'd be dressed in white or be as clean as these two men were.

"Yes, we are," Rueben shouted back. "Come on ashore. We were marooned when our ship, *The Queen*, sank during the hurricane."

The man shook his head. "You'll have to come out to us. We'll get stuck if we come any closer. Would you like for us to take you to the nearest port? Our captain has sent us to offer his assistance."

"Of course," Adelida yelled, advancing toward the edge of the water, her skirttails dragging in the sand.

"If you will come out to our lifeboats, we'll be glad to take you," the man rowed a little closer when he saw how pretty the lady was.

"I want to take my trunk," she said.

"I don't know about that," the man said.

"I won't leave without it. A lady has to have clothing, even to the next port," she said.

"Yes, ma'am, I can see that you would," he said. "If you will help me, sir?"

Rueben moaned, but closed the trunk lid and pushed it out into the water, expecting it to sink at any second. Surprising enough, it floated right to the boat as if it had a mind of its own. Rueben helped the big man lug it over the side of the small boat, both of them panting before they got it loaded.

"What's in that thing? Iron bullets?" The man laughed.

"Silverware. Weighs a ton. Washed up to shore in that big old closet over there," Rueben explained honestly. "She decided she wanted to keep it since she lost everything of her own in the storm."

"I see. Well, I'd say you'd best carry your wife out here

or those skirt tails will weigh as much as this trunk," he said, with a chuckle.

Rueben steeled himself for the sparks when she laced her arms around his neck. He was not disappointed. The feathery touch of her fingertips on his skin filled him with heat. He looked down into her eyes, forgetting there were two men sitting in lifeboats out in the shallows. For a moment they were the only two people left on Earth, stranded on an island forever. He leaned forward and brushed a kiss across her lips, setting off an explosion in both their hearts.

"Stop celebrating the rescue and come on," the other man yelled. "We ain't got all day. Got to make it to the next port by nightfall."

"Don't let that happen again," Adelida whispered.

"Just making sure they know you are my wife. It didn't mean a thing," he said stiffly. "I don't want you telling them about the treasure and them tying me to an anchor and dropping me over the side of the ship."

"Well, I'm glad it didn't mean a thing. It was repulsive to me," she lied. Two minutes after the kiss, her heart still raced, thumping against her breast so hard she thought it would jump right out into the ocean.

"Who are you?" the man asked, as he took Adelida from Rueben's arms and set her firmly on the floor of the boat beside her precious trunk.

"Rueben Hamilton, and this is my wife, Adelida," he said, as he took the proffered arm and swung himself up into the boat.

"Pleased to make your acquaintance. We are from *The Ambassador*, a passenger and mail ship headed for Savannah, Georgia. We'll port for mail for a couple of hours at supper time," the man began to row back toward the ship after he motioned for his partner to go on ahead of him. "He'll get there first and tell the captain that there were only the two of you. We've seen signs of more than one wrecked ship. The hurricane must've hit about a day before we arrived in the area from the looks of things. Saw some bodies, pardon me, ma'am," he tipped his straw hat in reverence.

She nodded seriously toward the man.

"I'm Frank Simmons, first mate to the captain. I do believe there is one empty stateroom if you all are interested in going to Savannah," he said.

"We would be glad to visit with the captain about arrangements," Rueben said. "We were on our way from Louisiana to Baltimore. I just finished an enlistment in the army."

"Down there for the Reconstruction?" Frank asked.

"That's right," Rueben said.

"And you are a Southern lady?" Frank asked.

"Born and raised on the bayou. But I let this soldier talk me into marriage and am going to the mountains in Pennsylvania with him," Adelida said, her soft southern drawl dripping pure honey and mesmerizing poor old Frank.

"Well, today is your lucky day," Frank nodded. "You'll be aboard a fine ship and we'll take good care of you. Good thing you had that fire built. It was the smoke that caught our eye. We never go near those little islands most usually. Too shallow for boats to get in and out."

"You are so kind," Adelida said, barely above a whisper.

She was good, Rueben had to give her that much.

An hour later, they were standing before the captain in the most luxurious surroundings Adelida had ever seen—mahogany-paneled walls, shiny yet soft looking and a desk the size of the armoire they'd left on the sand bar, with papers arranged in neat stacks all over it.

"You were lucky to survive such a storm," the gray-haired man told them. "And smart to keep such a big fire going on the banks. That's what drew us to you. You are welcome to ride on the top deck until evening when we stop for mail at the next port of call."

"We would rather book passage to Savannah," Rueben said. "My wife," he almost choked on the word, "was wise enough to keep some money tucked safely inside her garments, so we can pay."

"We only have one suite of rooms left to offer. The most expensive on the ship. A nice sitting room, private bath area, big four poster bed and fireplace in case the evenings are cool," the captain said. "That room to Savannah goes for five hundred dollars."

"Then we shall have it," Adelida said. "Could I borrow the area behind that screen?"

"Why, yes, ma'am, you surely may," the captain nodded.

She pulled the threads from the little pocket inside her camisole and extracted five hundred dollars from her stash. Rueben would give back half of it when they divided up the rest of the cash hiding in the bottom of the trunk, and she would definitely keep tally of how much his portion was, and since they hadn't found it necessary to use the silver for passage, she was laying claim to it, too.

"I believe that is five hundred dollars," she laid out the bills before him. "How many days is it to Savannah?"

"Five," the captain counted the money and made a receipt in his book for it. "We'll dock late this evening for a couple of hours. Then we'll be aboard the ship for two solid days and nights. The next stop for us is St. Augustine. If all goes well and there's not another hurri-cane, we'll be there just after noon on the third day and stop for a couple of hours. The next day we'll stop at supper time and give you all an hour to walk on dry land. The following day right after breakfast we reach our destination, which is Savannah."

"And if we wish to go on to Baltimore?" Rueben asked.

"You'll have to find another ship. Savannah is where we reload and go back," the captain said. "Did you hit your head in the storm? Your wife did a fine job of stitching you," he pointed to the black stitches on Rueben's forehead.

"No, he thought he was big and mean enough to stop a bank robbery with a single gun," Adelida said. "One of the three robbers hit him on the head with his shotgun."

"In New Orleans?" the captain eyed him carefully. "About a week ago?"

"That's right," Adelida said.

"I read about that robbery in the paper. So you're the man," he grinned.

"I suppose so," Rueben said. "Do you suppose we might go on to our suite now? I'm sure my wife would like to have a bath and refresh herself. And could we please have some food? Maybe some leftovers from the lunch that was served?"

"Yes, of course," he said.

"Thank you," Adelida murmured.

"Yes, thank you for rescuing us," Rueben said. "We were afraid we'd be on that island until we were old and gray."

"One of our guests spotted your fire when he was using his spy glass to hunt for strange birds. The island is way off the beaten path. Only old-time pirates went near them. Oh, and scavengers who'll be along shortly to work the wreckage of the storm. I'm sure you would have been found before you were old and gray," he guided them toward the door.

"Where exactly are we?" Rueben asked.

"One minute, I'll show you on the map." The captain stopped and pulled down a huge map from a bar on the wall. "We are right here. Those little dots are the islands. There are thousands of them. The one you were on is this one. I've been interested for years in the old pirates' tales. Don't suppose you found any journals or such on the island?"

"We found oranges, coconuts, clams, and lots of sand," Adelida said. "But not a single journal. Of course, we weren't looking for such things. We were more interested in potatoes and onions."

"I see," the captain said. "Well, those old pirates a hundred years ago hid their treasures somewhere down here. Someday some of it will be found, I'm sure. I'd just like to see their journals. I'm sure they'll be worth as much or more than what they hid."

"I'm sure, also," Rueben agreed. While Adelida skipped around the truth, Rueben had quickly followed the longitude and latitude lines and got a fix on the exact island they were on and committed it to memory. When they reached Savannah, he would tell Reed, and by the time he got home to Love's Valley, all six of those chests would be in Hamilton hands.

"Such a long way from anything and in such dangerous seas," Rueben said. "We are grateful to you for taking the time to save us."

"You are quite welcome," the captain opened the door, caught the nearest steward and gave him rapid instructions about where to put the Hamiltons. He nodded seriously and led them across the highly-polished dining room floor to a set of double doors, which he threw open with a flourish.

Adelida could have melted into the floor in a heap of pure gratitude when she saw the big brass tub in the enclosed bathroom. But she almost wept in happiness when she realized there were two rooms, separated by a door, each with an enormous bed covered with a white spread and pillows propped up at the headboard.

"So we each have our own," Rueben said.

"For a hundred dollars a day, they should be gold plated," Adelida said as the steward dragged their chest into the room.

"Shall I unpack?" the steward asked.

"No thank you," Adelida said. "But if you have a ship's store on board, we could use a few things. My husband," she was getting used to the word, "could use a pair of shoes or boots and some trousers that fit."

"Sorry, we can't help you," the steward said. "But there is a general store in the next port of call where he can find those things. It's only a one-store place right now. Could possibly grow into a town, but I don't see it happening. Now I'll go hustle some food."

"No fish," she said.

He laughed. "I can understand that, ma'am."

"And no more of those kisses," Adelida turned on Rueben when the doors were closed. "And I mean it. We aren't married, not really, and we won't ever be. So don't you go acting like it except when we are in public, and no kisses even then."

"Don't you worry. I couldn't make myself kiss you again."

Chapter Nine

"Oh, sit still. It's not going to hurt," Adelida said, her patience with Rueben waxing thin.

"How do you know? Have you ever had stitches removed?" Besides, there were different kinds of hurt involved in removing two stitches. There was the primary pain, that of having those stitches yanked free of the skin. Then there was the secondary pain, that of having someone who looked and smelled like Adelida touching him.

"Yes, I have. Got a fish hook, a big one, in my arm one time and my mama had to sew it up. I was five and I didn't carry on like you're doin'. If you don't let me take those out they're going to infect. It's been ten days, Rueben, and the doctor said . . ."

He cut her off mid-sentence. "The doctor also supposedly said I wasn't to sleep with you until I got my memory, at which time I would remember we weren't married and then you'd be safe. Right?"

"Hush," she snapped. "If you don't let me take them out then we can't go to supper, and if I have to stay

103

cooped up in this room with you another day, I'm going to use these scissors to cut your handsome throat."

Had she called him handsome? She had. Yes, indeed, she had. Without even realizing it, she'd said it. "Okay, go ahead and take them out now." He closed his eyes. He darned sure didn't want to see those sharp scissors coming at him. Even if she did deem him handsome, she might change her mind and plunge them into his heart or his eye just to get even for the day.

It hadn't started out so bad. They'd docked the evening before for a couple of hours. He'd felt pretty foolish walking into the general store with no shoes, but when the story was revealed that he and Adelida had survived the hurricane, the owner of the store was very sympathetic and helpful. Rueben bought trousers and a pair of good boots. They didn't have a single piece of women's clothing, so Adelida had bought a bolt of calico, some extra thread and buttons. She'd spent the whole day spitting out Cajun words that Rueben was sure he didn't want to understand. By mid-afternoon, after he'd had a nice long nap and read a couple of newspapers, she'd declared quite emphatically that they weren't staying in the room for supper. She was going out to the dining room even if she did look like someone's servant.

"Now was that so painful?" she asked, holding the spidery looking stitches in her palm for him to see. "In a year's time you won't even be able to see the scar."

He opened his eyes. Surely the stitches were bigger than those two little knot-looking things. They'd felt like six-inch sections of three-corded rope when they were in his head. Maybe they shrunk into nothing as she removed them. Or maybe she deftly cut away the foot-long sections of thread, and when he opened his eyes only the pitiful little knot remained.

"Pretty small to put up such a fuss over," she giggled and tossed them into a small trash can at the end of the desk.

"Let's go to supper. All I hear for hours and hours is moaning and groaning about getting something ready to wear so you can be presentable, and now you want to stand here and argue about my stitches. I've been trying to get you to take them out all day. Don't know why you waited until evening when it was time to eat, and besides I'm starving."

"What you are full of would turn your eyes even darker brown," she said. Was Rueben Hamilton flirting with her? And worse yet, was she flirting back? She looked in the mirror above the vanity. Her cheeks were flushed nice and pink and a twinkle lit her brown eyes. Yes, they had been flirting. She'd have to watch that more closely.

"Why are you tucking that into your skirt?" he asked, referring to the jewel-handled dagger.

"Because I don't have a gun," she told him.

"But Adelida, you are on a ship that caters to passengers, not pirates. You don't need to take that with you to supper. Put it back in the trunk," he said.

"No, I'm taking it. Really, Rueben, I am. But not because I don't have a gun. Rather because I was foolish in bringing it off the island and don't want to leave it in the room. They know we were on the island. We were honest about the silver in the top of the trunk, but those men might come in here while we're at supper and find the dagger. One look and they'll know it's ancient and the jewels are real. They'll start to wonder. I made a small pocket inside the folds of my skirt. It won't ever be seen, I promise," she said.

When they walked into the dining room all eyes were on them. Adelida figured it was because they were the rescued couple. Rueben knew the real reason was because Adelida was so beautiful. In her yellow cotton skirt and creamy-colored shirtwaist, she was dressed plainer than any woman in the elaborate dining room, and was still more beautiful. His heart swelled with pride . . . for a minute.

"Ah, the Hamiltons," a steward appeared at their side. "Captain Gilford has asked you to have dinner at his table. This way, please."

"Oh, my," Adelida mumbled.

Rueben didn't know if she was worried about her simple attire or if there was a remote possibility his hand on the small of her back had some kind of effect on her. He hoped it was the latter and that she'd discovered an attraction to him that she would have to battle, just like the one he had to fight. Surely it was just the result of kissing death right smack on the lips and living to tell the story, of sharing that kind of experience and cheating the Grim Reaper out of their souls during the hurricane.

"Good evening," Captain Gilford stood, waiting until Rueben had seated Adelida before he sat back down. "Thank you for joining me. You certainly are lovely this evening, Mrs. Hamilton."

"Thank you," she nodded formally.

"Allow me to introduce myself," the elderly lady beside Adelida said. "I'm Minnie Green from Savannah, Georgia. I'm coming back from New Orleans with my sister. Quite a journey for a woman my age, but it's been exciting. I'm just so glad we didn't get shipwrecked by that hurricane. I understand you and your handsome husband barely survived it with nothing but the clothes on your back."

"I'm pleased to make your acquaintance, ma'am,"

Adelida said. "And yes, the ship we were on did sink. We were among the last ones put into a lifeboat. There were times the rain and the waves were both so fierce I couldn't tell which was which."

"Why, you are a Southern girl," Minnie patted her arm. "Where you from, darlin'?"

"New Orleans most recently. That's where I met my husband, Mr. Hamilton. But I'd only lived there a few weeks. I was raised up on the Bayou Penchant in Acadia. Over around Terrebonne Parish," she said.

"And you, Mr. Hamilton? Are you from Louisiana also?" Minnie asked.

"No madame, I am not. I'm from southern Pennsylvania. We're on our way back there," he said, wondering if he should cross his fingers under the table. He had no intention of taking Adelida to Love's Valley. Not even for a few days while they settled up their finances. Not even if he had to stay in Savannah until the treasure was discovered and all the banking done to share it with the smart-mouthed Cajun.

"A Yankee and a rebel," Minnie's eyes, set in a bed of wrinkles, twinkled. "Now that should make for some mighty interesting arguments in the next few months."

"Next few months!" Adelida exclaimed. "It already has."

"They say opposites attract each other," Minnie said. "But you two better love each other a whole bunch, darlin'. It's a tough old world right out there at this time of history for a Southern girl and a Yankee to be getting married. Can't say as I could do it even if I was a young girl with a heart full of love and a brain full of mush. Ah, here's our dinner. I'll eat and stop prattling about matters that are none of my business."

Dinner was served in courses, starting with a nice thick clam chowder chocked full of potatoes, onions and celery, seasoned just right with a big, hot, fluffy yeast roll on the side. That alone could have been the entire meal, but Adelida didn't turn away the fish fillet, rolled in corn meal with just a touch of cayenne pepper and fried crisp, served with steamed rice and sweet carrots. Dessert was a thin slice of apple pie with coffee—black and almost strong enough to suit her tastes.

"And now that the meal is finished, may I ask you to dance, Mrs. Hamilton?" Captain Gilford stood and offered his arm.

There was no getting out of it. He'd asked them to sit at his table like royalty and now the price had been delivered. She'd have to dance with him. It didn't mean so much, she told herself as he led her out to the middle of the dance floor. The band played a slow waltz that Adelida didn't recognize. It sure didn't sound like bayou music and there wasn't a single washboard or set of spoons, not even a juice box up there amongst the violins and piano.

"You dance beautifully. Did your governess teach you these steps?" Captain Gilford asked.

"No, my brothers did," she bit her tongue. Adelida Broussau with a governess! Now, wasn't that enough to bring on a set of giggles.

"You aren't really married are you?" he asked out of nowhere.

For a split second she hesitated. Hopefully not long enough for him to realize she'd shifted from sweet little bayou girl to her poker playing mode. "Why would you ask such a silly question?" She purposely leaned back and looked him right in the eye without so much as a flutter of eyelashes.

"I have it from a very good source who was standing

outside your open window today that you were cussing Rueben in your native tongue and at one time you said something about being glad you weren't really married to him. Besides, newlyweds don't act like you two do. It just doesn't fit, Mrs. Hamilton. You don't act married. You act like friends or maybe cousins who tolerate each other," he said.

"You are wrong. All women are not mealymouthed little flowers. Some of us speak our minds and what your informant heard was quite possibly me telling him I didn't know why I'd married him, not that I wasn't really married to him," she said. "But just for conversation's sake, if you were right, what difference would it make?"

"I am a married man, Mrs. Hamilton, but I'm away from home for months at a time. It's not unusual for me to indulge myself at times when the opportunity presents itself. Do you understand what I'm offering you, should I be right about your marital status?" he asked, careful not to draw her any closer into the embrace of the dance than he would a bonafide, married young lady.

"Yes, I think I do, but you are wrong. Rueben and I come from very different backgrounds and we are both hot-tempered, but we will survive the storms of getting used to each other just like we did the hurricane," she said.

"Well, should you change your mind about being married, I would be most glad to open my door and find you on the other side of it any one of the next three nights. I don't make it a habit of indulging myself with married women. It can make for some messy situations when there's nothing but sea all around and no place to escape an irate husband. If you should decide you aren't really married, I could offer you a return trip to your homestate free of charge and accommodations of the best sort," he said.

"But you, sir, are a married man. You have a wife at home and children?" She raised an eyebrow.

"Five children. Three sons and two lovely daughters," he said.

"And you would cheat on your wife and disgrace your children?"

"You are an innocent," he chuckled. "My wife and children will never be touched by what I do at sea. All men are alike. If you are indeed married, keep Rueben Hamilton close by your side or you'll always wonder now, won't you?"

Adelida drew back her hand and slapped him soundly, leaving a red mark on his cheek. She had the dagger removed from the pocket of her skirt and pointed at his Adam's apple before he had time to raise his hand to his burning face.

"Adelida, what are you doing?" Rueben raced to her side.

"This sorry excuse for a man has made indecent advances toward me. Don't worry, Rueben. You won't have to call him out to a duel. I'll cut his throat right here," she whispered in red hot anger.

"My apologies, Mr. Hamilton," the captain eyed the dagger. "I'm afraid your wife took what I said in the wrong way. However, I do apologize and assure you it will not happen again. Now, please, put away that knife."

Women had begun to point and gasp. Men were gazing at what appeared to be a fight between the captain and the pretty young wife of the rescued couple.

"Go back to your dancing," the captain reached out and pushed Adelida's hand back. "It's a minor misunderstanding."

"I would hope that you are right," Rueben said tightly,

taking the dagger from Adelida's shaking hands. "We will be retiring to our room now, where my wife is going to tell me what you have said."

"Keep in mind, Mrs. Hamilton, that the whole conversation was merely a hypothetical situation. I did not mean to offend you in the least. I am afraid your dear wife may have suffered from too much sun," the captain tried to cover his horrendous mistake as he slithered away into the crowd of dancing people.

"Get me out of here. I want off this ship as soon as possible," Adelida said, as he led her to her room. Was the captain right? Were all men so fickle? If so, she'd never fall in love. But how did a woman know, really know down deep in her heart, which ones would make good husbands and which ones were pure skunks?

Tomorrow they'd be on the ship all day and she would beg off eating in the dining room that evening. The next day they'd have two stops, one in St. Augustine for three hours in the morning and one at supper time. The morning after that they would be in Savannah. She'd stay in her room until then.

"What happened?" Rueben asked the minute he'd shut the door to the room.

Adelida put a forefinger to her lips and shook her head ever so slightly. "Why sugar, I've sewed and fought with you all day. I've worn my lovely little outfit and now I'm ready to make up with you for all the arguing. That's the only beauty of a rousing good fight—the making up," she said, as she went straight to the open window. She stood perfectly still long enough to see a small puff of smoke float out to sea. So the captain's spy was standing with his back to the ship's wall, right beside the window. And now that she'd let her anger get ahead of her and shown them the dagger, they'd know there was either treasure on the island or else she was a very rich woman to own an artifact like that.

"The good captain propositioned me. He said he knew we weren't married because we didn't act like a married couple, and that if he was right I could come to visit him in his room tonight or any time I wanted," she whispered into Rueben's ear so quietly the spy could not possibly hear it. "I lost my temper. Now he has someone outside the window to listen to what we say."

"What?" Rueben cocked his head to one side, his brow furrowing in a scowl and the ever so slight dimple in his chin deepening.

She motioned with her finger for him to come to her. She frowned and made a more definite motion, setting her mouth in a firm line and pointing toward the window. She showed him another puff of smoke filtering out to sea followed by a slight sigh. She wrapped her arms around his neck. "Kiss me loud and long. Tell me that you are sorry the captain was rude and that you will humor me and we will stay in our room for the rest of the journey," she whispered. "Then tell me you love me and that it's time to shut the window and turn in for the night."

"I'd rather tell you that I was going to stab him in his bed," he whispered back.

"No, the spy has to report that you aren't going to do anything or they'll kill us for sure," she mouthed close to his ear.

He drew back, looked deep into her big brown eyes and did just what she'd asked. Never let it be said a Hamilton man wasn't willing to kiss a woman when she just stood up there and asked for it outright. His brothers would have both been ashamed of him if he'd let an opportunity like that pass.

She leaned into his arms and melted into the kiss. It would certainly be easy to fall prey to what a kiss like that could lead into. But Adelida wasn't a fool. The captain had just said all men were alike in their thinking. She'd keep her heart chained down tight and throw away the key. There was no way she would spend her life wondering if her husband was offering a woman entry into his bed while she was sitting at home with five kids.

"Darling, you are shivering. Let me shut the window and we'll turn in early tonight. I'll brush your hair for you. Perhaps that will ease the headache. Are you sure the captain compromised you?" he drew away from her reluctantly.

"Yes, but perhaps he really was only flirting and I took it all wrong," she said loud enough that the spy beside the window heard.

When the window was shut, Rueben followed Adelida into her bedroom. "Now tell me exactly what that rascal said to you!"

"I'm tired now and I really am going to retire early. If you'll shut the door, please," she dismissed him with a flick of her wrist.

"No, Adelida, I won't," he plopped down on the side of her bed. "You'll tell me or I'll sleep in this bed with you."

He was handsome when he was mad, and that was a temptation to be sure, but Adelida wasn't giving in to temptations that night.

"Mon ami," she said. "I suppose we can be friends. We've been through a lot together and that makes for friendship. The captain saw through our story, and now he's seen the dagger really close so we'll be spied on constantly."

"I should call him out to a duel," Rueben said, his tone cold and hard.

"Of course you should if we were married but we
aren't," she reminded him. "He's just taking advantage of
what might be an opportunity. Telling me his bedroom
door was open if I should decide that I want to change my
mind and not be married after all . . . it's a mixed up
affair, isn't it? Since I let my anger get ahead of my good
sense, we'll be staying in our room tomorrow. Then the
next day we will be in St. Augustine, wherever that is, in
the morning and through the noon meal. Supper will be in
another port and the next morning we'll be in Savannah.
So it can be worked out. I wouldn't be surprised if the spy
came into our room and went through our things while we
were shopping at the last stop. We'll just have to stay in
the room and pretend it was all my fault, or I'm sure
they'll kill us, Rueben."

"I wonder why he didn't dance with one of the women
who . . ." Rueben felt the blush rising from the nape of his
neck.

"Who what?" Adelida asked.

"Who do that kind of thing for a living," Rueben said
in a rush. "There are at least two or three on the ship."

"And just how do you know that?" Adelida propped
both hands on her hips and glared at him.

"A man just knows, that's all. Those kind of women act
different than well-brought-up ladies or young married
women," he chose his words carefully, actually trying not
to offend her.

"So have you looked at one of those women?" she
asked, knowing fully well that if he did it wasn't one bit
of her business.

"No, Adelida, I have not. I've been a good husband
even if I'm not a husband. I just want to go home and forget all this."

"The first step toward you getting home is to go to your own room and be careful until we dock in Savannah," she said flatly. "I have a headache."

"Then I'll brush your hair. Sit down," he pointed toward the vanity.

She sat down before she thought and then wanted nothing more than to jump up the minute his hands began to search for the pins that kept her hair up. The kind of strain he was putting on her heart would certainly make her headache worse.

Chapter Ten

Savannah had escaped much of the destruction during the war. The cotton industry had rebounded, breathing life into the city, creating a pulse that reached out to Adelida even as she and Rueben left the ship. Relief washed over her. They had avoided the captain for three days even if they'd been spied on continually. She was confident that they'd convinced the spy they were only a young married couple on their way home, and that now the ordeal was over. She looked forward to shopping, prowling up and down the boardwalk, and setting her feet on solid ground.

People were hugging and kissing, oblivious to the fact that they were in public, hearts erasing social protocol. Rueben drew her close to his side, afraid she'd be swept away in the tide of human bodies, yet after three days of constant company with the Cajun, he almost wished she would disappear like a puff of smoke, never to be seen again. They'd argued. Ignored each other. Pretended. He was glad that it was over, and although a part of him liked the excitement, the staid side of Rueben was relieved to see Savannah. The end of the trail of subterfuge.

"Rueben!" a masculine voice shouted. "Over here, Rueben."

Rueben raised a hand, a grin covering his face as he edged his way toward his younger brother, Reed. Adelida was pulled through the masses, most of them taller than her petite five-feet-two inches.

"Man, I'm glad to see you," Rueben patted Reed's shoulder.

"And this is?" Reed looked down at the beautiful woman.

"This is . . ." Rueben said, but before he could finish, someone in the crowd shoved a man into his arm. He looked into Captain Gilford's eyes standing not more than a foot from him.

"I'm so sorry. That was an accident, I assure you. The rush of people is always like this when we reach port. Accept my apologies, Mr. Hamilton," the captain said seriously.

"Accepted," Rueben said curtly. "And Reed, this is my wife, Adelida."

"Hello, Reed," Adelida extended a hand. "I'm very glad to meet you."

"You rascal," Reed was practically breathless. "Momma is going to be surprised. Where are you from, Adelida?"

"Louisiana. Acadia. Terrebonne Parrish. The bayou," she said miserably, noting the captain still standing close enough to hear even if his back was turned.

"Mr. and Mrs. Hamilton, I trust that the rest of your journey won't involve hurricanes," Captain Gilford said.

"Or men who do not keep their priorities straight," Adelida said curtly.

"A simple misunderstanding," the captain tipped his hat at them.

"Married! I can't believe it. Married! First Monroe and then Ellie and now you. Looks like I'll be the only bachelor left at Indigo's wedding reception," Reed said.

The brothers talked. Adelida studied them both and kept an eye on the captain, who was having a conversation with one of the stewards, a man with a cigar. There was definitely a family resemblance between Reed and Rueben. They shared the same face structure, all angles, and the same slight dimple in their chin, but there were differences, too. Reed had lighter hair, bordering on dishwater blond, and his eyes were the clearest blue she'd ever seen. A handsome man that would turn any bayou girl's head for a second glance, but not nearly as handsome as Rueben.

"Rueben, sugar, could we continue our visit with Reed at the hotel? I'm very tired and also very hungry," Adelida said.

"I'm sorry, Adelida. I'm just so glad to see family that I've been rude. My plans will have to be changed," Reed laughed and patted his brother on the back. "I'd planned on Rueben staying at my quarters, but that won't work with a wife. There's a really nice hotel at the end of this street. We can easily walk there, but wait, do you have baggage?"

"One trunk. Left it in our stateroom until we found you," Rueben said. "Suppose we could carry it off and catch transportation to the hotel?" Damnation! He sure hadn't planned on having to tell his brother a lie, most especially one of such magnitude.

Cigar smoke followed them back to the ship. It was just a whiff now and then, but it was enough to heighten Adelida's senses. "Our friend continues to follow us," she said softly so that only Rueben heard. "Be very careful

what you say. The captain talked to him after he so rudely bumped into you."

"So what do you think of our sister marrying Tommy?
Who'd a thought those two would ever get together! He's
so quiet and slow-talking. I've always seen her needing a
man with as much temper as she's got," Reed said, ignoring Adelida's whispering.

"To be honest, I was shocked when I got the letter
telling me she was seeing Tommy. They're as mismatched
a couple as I've ever seen," Rueben laughed. "But I'll tell
you the truth, Reed, you could have blown me over with a
chicken feather when I heard our brother Monroe had
married a Texan. He was so bitter the last time we saw
him, I didn't think anyone or anything would ever get
through his hard heart."

"Me too," Reed said. "That was an even bigger shock-
er than when I got the news that Ellie had married a rebel.
No offense now, Adelida. You'll understand when you get
home and understand her circumstances."

"None taken. The war is over. We need to get on with
life," she said, not knowing where her crazy mind had
dragged those words from. "Here's our chest, and then
can we please get off this ship? I'm ready for solid
ground."

"I can understand that. What you got in this thing? Pure
gold?" Reed asked when he picked up the leather strap on
one end.

A thin stream of smoke blew across the doorway to
their stateroom.

"Of course not," Adelida said. "But there is a lovely set
of silver in there. It washed up inside an old armoire on
the island where we were stranded. It was all we found of
value in there. There were a few women's dresses that

Rueben said we could make a tent out of they were so big."

Reed cocked his head to one side and stared at his new sister-in-law. Her eyebrows were drawn and she nodded toward the door. Something passed between her and Rueben that Reed couldn't understand. Twice in only a few minutes. His senses told him there was an underlying current that had nothing to do with being newlyweds.

"Well, let's get this heavy thing off the ship and into your room. Far be it from me to complain about carrying a lady's silver," Reed said.

"There's something I need to discuss with you," Rueben whispered under his breath as they loaded the trunk onto the first taxi on the dock.

"And what would that be?" Reed asked, stepping back to let Rueben and Adelida into the buggy before him.

"Well, hello," Adelida said, a bit too loudly. "Are you as glad to be on dry ground as I am? Will you have a few days before you have to start back to New Orleans?"

The steward grinned, showing off a wide space between his front teeth. "Yes, I am and yes, I will have a couple of days. And you would be the . . . too many people, I do forget names easily."

"The Hamiltons. Remember, we're the ones who were rescued from the island. We survived the hurricane. You rowed out in the second boat to rescue us and got back to the ship before we did to make them aware of what had happened," she said sweetly, fanning her skirttails out. The seats were narrow so Rueben's shoulder touched hers, making her wish she could pick up those same skirt-tails and fan the blistering heat away from her face.

"Now you had something to talk to me about?" Reed asked.

"Yes, I do," Rueben said. "Do we buy a set of silver

flatware for our sister's wedding present or do we start building her a new house?"

"Does Tommy want to live in the country? He's lived in town his whole life. Maybe Indigo would rather go to Shirleysburg than live in Love's Valley," Reed said. Something wasn't right. The urgency that had been in Rueben's tone didn't warrant something as simple as a wedding present.

"I don't think Tommy has much to do with where they'll live. If Indigo ain't happy, ain't nobody happy. Tommy better have already learned that before we get home or he's in for one rude awakening," Rueben laughed.

"That's not just Indigo. It's all women," Reed chuckled.

"Oh, is it now?" Adelida's temper flared.

"Settle down, sweetheart," Rueben slipped his arm around her shoulders and pulled her closer to him. Just to throw the steward off-course, he told himself, enjoying the way she fit so well in the crook of his arm. "When you meet Indigo you'll see what we're talking about. She's very opinionated and speaks her mind. Not a whole lot unlike you."

The steward grinned broadly, enjoying the show immensely. "And where are you newlyweds staying tonight?" he asked.

The hair on the back of Rueben's neck prickled. "At whatever hotel where my brother here can find us a nice room."

"Just down the street a little ways," Reed said. "We could have walked, but my sister-in-law has silver knives and forks that weigh a ton so we didn't want to carry the trunk. And you sir, where are you staying?"

"Oh, perhaps the same hotel if they have a room. I'm looking forward to a real bed tonight instead of a berth.

Our ship will reload tomorrow morning and we'll be returning to New Orleans," he said.

"Well, here we are," Reed said. "Good luck on your return voyage. Hopefully there won't be any more hurricanes. Did you know there's been a dozen ships lost in one way or another this past month?"

"Comforting thought," the steward said, turning to Rueben and Adelida. "And I bid you two good luck on the rest of your journey home and may your sister's temper be sweetened by the time you get there."

"Thank you," Rueben said.

"If you're nice to me," Adelida looked right at Rueben, "then my temper might get sweeter too. Now, come on and feed this Cajun. I told you when the Broussaus get hungry we get meaner than a swamp 'gater."

"Yes, ma'am," he said. "Reed and I'll take this trunk up to our room and then we'll . . ."

"Why, here, fellers, let me help with that trunk. I remember it weighs a ton from when we brought it on board. Three strong backs will make it easier," the steward offered.

Twenty minutes later, the Hamiltons and the steward were both standing in the middle of a very nice bedroom—with one bed taking center stage. The steward had managed to acquire the room next door.

"So Mrs. Hamilton, you might need to put cotton in your ears if you hear me snoring in the next room. I tend to do that when I'm away from the ship," the steward teased, as he stepped back out into the hallway.

"It can't be any louder than Rueben," she said lightly. "Perhaps I should find a room in another hotel."

The steward chuckled and waved. They heard the door to his room close softly and the window being raised.

"Shhhh," Adelida put her finger to her mouth and

shushed both men when they opened their mouths to speak. "Later. Let's go to the dining room, and I'll lay you dollars to swamp rats that that steward is right behind us before we even get down the stairs," she whispered.

Reed looked at both of them. "I think it's time for you to tell me what is going on."

"Darling," Rueben cut in, looking right at Reed but talking to Adelida who was halfway across the room. "Must you primp and preen before the mirror? You said you were hungry. Goodness knows they'll have all the food eaten before we even get to the dining room if you don't hurry."

"A woman can't be expected to go to dinner all wind-blown. There now. That's perfect. Give me one more minute to wash some of the sea dust from my face," Adelida said, her voice carrying out the open window and her finger pointing toward the thin stream of smoke wafting inside the room.

"Rueben, write down those numbers," she wrote on a piece of hotel stationary. Thinking that the captain would be content to leave matters alone once they reached Savannah had been silly. He'd probably watch them closer now than ever before.

Her fingers brushed Rueben's when she handed him the paper. She'd done that many times the past few days and it never failed to set his heart aflame.

Reed's face showed nothing but bewilderment.

Rueben wrote the longitude and latitude of the island on the paper and a very quick note saying that one of the Hamilton ships needed to go there immediately to recover treasure hidden close to the cistern in a cellar covered with sand. He ended by saying that the steward was a spy and listening to everything they said.

"Come on, Adelida. For goodness sake, anyone as

beautiful as you doesn't need to primp so long. Now I'm hungry and a hungry Hamilton is meaner than a Love's Valley mountain lion with a whole passel of cubs," he said as Reed read the note, light finally dawning in his face.

"I'm ready," Adelida said. "Let's go, but after we eat I want to come back up here and let Reed look at my silver forks and spoons. They're quite lovely and someday I'm going to set a fine table with them in Love's Valley. You can bring your wife and have dinner with us when you get married, and we'll tell her story of our rescue from the island. You know, I still wish I could have figured a way to get that armoire off the island. Rueben says it wouldn't ever be worth a dime because the wood had swollen, but it was so pretty. Do you have a lady friend, Reed?" She kept up a running monologue until they were in the hallway and only winked briefly at Rueben when the steward was suddenly right behind them.

"No, I do not, and I'm not looking for a lady friend either. I'm going to be the bachelor at Indigo's wedding. The one she won't be mad at for bringing a rebel spouse home," Reed chuckled.

"Be careful," Adelida teased. "You're treading on dangerous ground there. Well, look here, who is right behind us. Hello, again," she said over her shoulder. "Are you going down to dinner? Then please join us. We'd be glad to have you. Reed will tell us what's the best food on the menu, won't you?"

"Of course," Reed said, admiring Adelida.

They talked of the hurricane and the rescue, of the island and how they'd had a clam dig, gigged a huge snook for supper one night, and had eaten coconuts and oranges. Adelida carefully drew the steward into the conversation as much as she could, getting him to tell his experience in keeping a whole ship of passengers calm while they endured the fringes of the storm, as well as how amazed he was that the rescue boat didn't sink under the weight of that trunk. An hour later, she yawned, covering her mouth quite daintily with her hand.

"I'm afraid I will have to leave you gentlemen to talk of wars and rumors of wars, ships and shipwrecks, while I go upstairs to have a nap. Reed, don't forget you were going to look at my silverware before you leave, remember? Rueben can show it to you when you gentlemen have finished your visit."

"I think I might join you," Rueben said. "Would you excuse us, sir?"

The steward was on his feet so fast he had to set the chair aright. "That sounds like a good plan to me, also. Good food does make a man sleepy, don't it?"

Reed said, "I'll take a look at that silver, but then I must get back to the fort until evening. I have you booked on . . ." he paused. "What is the name of that ship? Ah, yes, the *Princess*. I'll write down your departure time and the ship's name when we get to the room. You'll have tomorrow to take in the sights of Savannah, but I'm afraid I won't be free to show you around. But maybe we could have supper together before you leave," he said, as all four of them worked their way around white linen-covered tables.

"Have a nice rest then," the steward said, shutting the door to his bedroom. In barely a minute, Adelida could see the tell-tale smoke drifting out the window, not five feet away.

"The *Princess* at eight o'clock in the morning the day after tomorrow," Reed said, all the time writing, *The Virginia, seven o'clock tomorrow morning, and I'll meet you at the River Restaurant for supper.*

"I can remember that very well since I'm married to a Cajun princess," Rueben said.

"Oh, Reed, come and see my silver treasure," Adelida sounded like a parrot or even worse, a poor actress in a silly play. But she was quickly running out of things she could say with the spy in the very next room. She set the chest of silver on the floor and began tossing out clothing, letting it land where it would. Rueben's shortalls against the door, her own undergarments against the far wall, dresses in a heap on the bed. Then she pulled up the false bottom of the trunk, drew out a fist full of gold coins and handed them to Reed.

Rueben picked up a diamond necklace and put it in his hands. "What do you think, Reed? Do you think you could find something similar to this here in Savannah to give to Indigo for her wedding gift? Adelida liked it so much she's insisted on bringing it all the way home with her, so I'm sure Indigo would like some like it."

"Oh, I think I possibly could." Reed's eyes glittered as he peered into the chest.

How do we get it out of here? Adelida wrote on a piece of paper. If she never had to converse with a pen and paper again, she'd die a happy woman.

Supper time. I'll be back. You two go on to the River Restaurant without me, he wrote. "Yes, Adelida, I see why you wanted to save it. Would be a shame to leave something so lovely on a deserted island. And I do think Indigo would be very happy with a set just like it."

Extra key? he wrote. *I'll lock the door and leave it with the desk clerk.*

"Well, let's hope so," Adelida said. "We surely wouldn't want anyone to be unhappy at her wedding, now would we?"

"I'll go now," Reed said loudly, pocketing a handful of the coins and the diamond necklace. "I'll see you at the restaurant for supper then."

He was gone before either Rueben or Adelida could tell him they weren't really married. "We didn't tell him . . ." Rueben started and then stopped, staring at the window.

"What?" Adelida cut in.

"Nothing," Rueben stopped.

"That we hope he truly finds someone to love him as much as I do you, sugar?" she said, in her sweet Cajun drawl. "Or that his favorite old dog, Peaches, died?"

"He'll be sad when he hears about Peaches. He's had that dog for fifteen years. You can't know how much he liked the old boy, so don't be so sarcastic about it," Rueben said. The play acting was back. Even though it was exciting, he was growing tired of it.

She heard a faint chuckle float through the window. So the spy thought that was funny, did he?

"I'm so sorry. I didn't mean to be sarcastic. Come and lay down beside me. When we wake we'll go have a bite of supper with your brother. Who knows, maybe that nice steward will join us again. I never did catch his name, did you? The other one that rowed us back to safety was named Frank, but I never heard this one's name. Doesn't matter. We'll never see him again, but it would be nice to at least know. We'll ask him if we happen to bump into him again. Strange, how he got a room in the same hotel as us, isn't it?" She pushed on the bed, making the springs squeak, then promptly sat down in the rocking chair.

Rueben pointed toward the bed.

She shook her head emphatically. She was not going to sleep with him. Not even a nap where he kept to his side of the bed. And if he insisted on sleeping in the bed tonight, she'd sleep in the rocking chair or on the floor under the window.

He stifled a chuckle, tossed his boots on the floor, and stretched out on the bed. In five minutes he was asleep.

She curled up on the settee and considered taking her part of the treasure and simply disappearing. She didn't know anything about selling jewels though, and any street urchin could take advantage of her. She also didn't know which way to go to the mountains and she was determined to see them.

She didn't know how long she'd slept, but she awakened with a start when Rueben touched her on the shoulder.

"Ah, sleeping beauty, it is time to go have supper with my brother," he said.

"Don't talk to me. I'm not awake yet. A hungry Cajun or a sleepy one can be dangerous," she sniffed at the window. Cigar smoke for sure. Their spy was awake.

"Have you given some thought about what you'd like to see and do tomorrow?" Rueben asked.

"I want to find a dressmaker's store and hopefully there will be something there that will fit me," she said. "I can't go to meet your mother in this skirt, made on the spur of the moment. I miss my pretty things that were washed out to sea."

Meet his mother! He almost choked just hearing those words.

Sure enough the steward showed up at the River Restaurant at the same time they did and Adelida invited him to have supper with them.

"I couldn't, ma'am," he said. "Isn't your brother meeting you here? You'll want to spend your time with him."

"Reed will be an hour late getting here. We're not to wait on him for the meal, so we'd be glad to have you join us," Rueben said. "We never did get your name, though. Adelida and I were discussing that in our room just before we fell asleep. It would be nice to know it so we can tell my family about you."

"My name is Vincent," he said, not knowing quite what

to do. To refuse them his company could look suspicious. So far, Vincent thought the captain had mush for brains. The couple had never mentioned anything about a hidden treasure, even if the captain did swear she'd held an ancient knife to his throat when they were dancing. When they talked of the island it was just the lady whining about leaving her armoire, which in Vincent's opinion showed that she wasn't nearly as hoity-toity as the captain thought. Then there was the sweet kissy stuff and soft whispers before they disappeared behind the closed doors to her bedroom. There wasn't one thing going on, in his opinion, but he'd play this out through the evening and then have a talk with Captain Gilford later.

"Then you'll have supper with us, Vincent?"

"Be glad to, ma'am, and thank you for the invitation," he said.

Reed appeared an hour later, a grin on his face and a story about a young officer who'd fallen in love with one of the local lasses. He had served his enlistment and was to board *The Princess* in two days, but the Southern lady's father had opposed the marriage which had taken place at the courthouse. The couple had fled on horseback with everyone in the barracks cheering them on.

The steward was laughing so hard, he didn't see the letters exchange hands under the table. Later, by the light of the candle in their room, Rueben and Adelida read Reed's letter together. It told them simply that the ship had already left for the island; the trunk was now much lighter so they couldn't let Vincent help carry it downstairs; what was in the trunk had been delivered to a reputable member of the Hamilton firm who would convert it into cash. The letter also told them to be careful on the way home to Love's Valley and to give the family his love. He'd see them all in a couple of months.

Rueben slapped his forehead. In his brief letter, telling Reed one more time about the island's location and how to find the cellar under the sand, he'd forgotten again to tell him that Adelida was not really his wife.

The next morning, when Vincent arose and went down to the dining room, he scanned the room for the Hamiltons, but they weren't there. He asked the desk clerk if they'd had breakfast sent to their room.

"No, are they friends of yours?" the clerk asked.

"Just acquaintances. I was one of the people who rescued them off a small island after a hurricane sunk their ship. We traveled together on *The Ambassador* and shared supper last night and planned to have breakfast this morning," Vincent hoped he sounded convincing.

"Oh, I see. Well, they left in a rush this morning so I suppose they forgot to leave you a note. They hired a hackney to take them to the docks. Seems the wife decided she wanted to go on home rather than shop," the clerk told him.

He ran to the docks and asked several people there about the ships that had left early that morning. Three had gone. Two to Baltimore. One to Philadelphia. None back to the west until later that morning. No, they had no idea who or how many passengers each one had.

Vincent went back to the hotel for breakfast. The captain would be disappointed that he'd let them slip through his fingers, but there was always Roger. That ruthless man might not be as good of a spy as Vincent, but he had no scruples about how to make people talk. If the captain was right, Roger would find out where the treasure was hidden, even if he had to kill the young married couple.

Chapter Eleven

Adelida had been dreaming of the armoire when the ship docked in Charleston, South Carolina a couple of hours before dawn. She slowly opened her eyes. Someday she was going to own a huge house with a fancy armoire in every bedroom. She fluffed her pillow and settled back into the very uncomfortable settee. When Reed booked passage on the ship he hadn't reckoned on Rueben having a wife so he'd only paid for a single room—with one bed. Rueben had half-heartedly offered to take the settee and give her the bed, but she'd vetoed the idea right away. It was no wider than two parlor chairs and the sight of all six feet of brawny man curled up on the thing was enough to give Adelida the giggles. She stretched, throwing one leg over the end of the settee, but couldn't go back to sleep.

Admitting that she liked that Yankee hadn't been easy, but they'd become good friends during the past few weeks. *Oh, well,* she thought with a heavy sigh, *at least 'like' isn't 'love.' It's easier to tell a plain old friend good-bye at the end of a journey than to send your heart off with a man who you'll never see again.* She winced at the thought of never seeing the man she loved again. *Love?* She couldn't love him. Not Rueben Hamilton, the man who made her want to argue and fight all the time.

Moon beams drifted through the open window and across the bed where Rueben pretended to be asleep. He'd spent most of the night staring at Adelida, trying to decide just what he did feel for the woman. Friendship? Camaraderie? When she opened her eyes, he closed his— almost all the way, anyway—and faked sleep. Tomorrow, they'd have a few hours in Charleston. The captain had encouraged everyone at the dinner table to take advantage of the opportunity to get off the ship, since it would be three days until they reached the next port of call, where only an hour was planned for the passengers to walk on the beaches.

Lord, why did she have to be a Southern woman? he asked God, without looking up toward the heavens.

"Your eyes are puffy. Did you have a bad night on that uncomfortable settee?" Rueben asked the next morning at breakfast.

"No, I did just fine. What are we doing today?" she asked, sipping her weak coffee.

"I thought we'd go to a few shops and see if there's any good clothing. There are several things I need. The general store left a good bit to be desired, and we scarcely had time to purchase anything in Savannah."

"Sounds lovely," she said, suddenly aware that the man at the table next to them was staring right at her and listening intently to their conversation. Was there another spy on this ship too?

"I should write Reed and explain that we aren't . . ." Rueben started.

She pushed back her chair so quickly that he stopped midsentence. "Oh, I forgot my reticule in the state room. Please come with me to fetch it."

"What?" Rueben frowned.

"Pop that last bit of biscuit in your mouth and let's go," she said. "We'll stop mid-morning and find a cup of coffee and something sweet to tide us over until lunch." She kept a watchful eye on the man who stared at them unabashedly. When they were halfway across the big dining room, he left his table and followed.

"What's going on?" Rueben asked bluntly when they reached their room.

"Oh, please don't be mad at me for dragging you away from the breakfast table. I just wanted a few minutes alone with you before we go shopping," she said sweetly, going to the open window. No smoke this time, but the same man was standing at the ship's rail, looking out over the ocean.

"Again?" Rueben mouthed.

She nodded.

"Why? Did you want to discuss buying new drawers and camisoles and didn't want to do it in public?" Rueben went into his play acting mode.

"Why, yes, that's the very reason. You know me entirely too well," she grimaced at him, her tone and expression as different as the North and South. "Since all my fine underthings were lost in the hurricane, I would like to buy some more, and I'm sure it would embarrass you if I mentioned such things in public. You'll probably turn red as a beet when I ask about them in the dressmakers establishment, but I was afraid your face would burst into flames out there in the dining room."

"It won't embarrass me to go to the dressmaker's. After all, I like pretty underthings too. Unwrapping a package is part of the fun of a present," he declared, a twinkle in his green eyes.

"Oh, sugar, you do make me blush," she slapped his arm. *You better be careful*, she mouthed silently.

He raised an eyebrow and laughed.

When they left their room the man followed them, apparently not caring if they were aware of him or not.

Charleston had suffered during the war years, but it was coming back to life. With a population of forty thousand, it offered dressmakers by the dozens. She and Rueben wandered through the main section of town, her arm looped through his as if they were indeed a newly-married couple out for an early summer stroll.

"He's back there," Adelida told Rueben as they stopped and checked one store window after the other. "He stops every time we do and pretends to be interested in something. But he's even worse at his job than the last one."

"Thank goodness. At least we don't have to watch for cigar smoke. Maybe he's only going to follow us or watch us as long as we're in Charleston."

"Let's hope so. This whole thing makes me nervous as a . . ." she giggled. She couldn't finish the sentence, not even if she had been posing as a wife who supposedly could say ribald things to her husband.

"As a what?" he grinned. "As a long-tailed cat in a room full of rocking chairs?"

"That's not what I was thinking. Look at that lovely dress. I want to go in this shop. That would be wonderful to wear when I meet your mother," she said seriously, not caring if the spy heard.

"You still determined on going to Love's Valley?" Rueben asked.

"Of course," Adelida pushed open the doorway to the dress shop. A little bell rang and brought a tall, gangly lady with a tape measure around her neck to the front parlor.

"Hello," Adelida said.

"Can I help you?" the lady asked dubiously. Neither the countrified lady nor the mister were dressed like the clientele who frequented her shop.

"I am Adelida Hamilton and this is my husband, Rueben. I'm afraid we were shipwrecked in the hurricane down in Florida and lost everything we had. I need to be outfitted from the skin out and my husband would like a private parlor to wait for me."

"And I'm Miss Frannie," the lady's countenance changed immediately. "You sir, are welcome to the husband's sitting parlor behind there. There are cookies on the table and I'll have Mavis bring you some coffee while we see what we can do for your wife. There are newspapers for you if you so desire."

"My thanks," Rueben said.

Adelida patted him on the arm and disappeared into another fitting room with Miss Frannie. He picked up a newspaper, but his mind wandered, trying to put a definite description on his feelings for Adelida. It was more than camaraderie. More than friendship. He *loved* the woman. He threw the newspaper down as if it was guilty of making him finally admit the truth. Now that was a fine pickle of a mess. He couldn't take her home and have peace in Love's Valley, and Rueben wanted peace in his life. *Do you really?* he argued with himself. *Or do you want Adelida? You cannot have both. Either it's one or the other, because she doesn't bring any resemblance of peace with her. She'll keep you alert and alive, and there won't be a humdrum day left for you this side of the grave.*

Adelida purchased three dresses and a navy blue traveling suit trimmed with white piping and sporting a love-ly white lawn shirtwaist to go with the jacket and sweep-ing skirt. She also chose four changes of underthings and a beautiful swishing satin petticoat. Miss Frannie had a small selection of leather shoes with buttons up the sides, so Adelida bought two pair, one black and one brown. When she slung back the velvet curtains to the husband's parlor, she wondered what was in the newspaper to make Rueben's expression so dark.

"I'm ready now," she said.

"It's about time," he snapped.

"What's the matter with you? Did the South win the war after all?"

"No, they did not. We won once and we'd do it again," he said testily. Peace. That's what he wanted. He'd just decided. He'd never admit his feelings so she'd never know. Besides, she couldn't love him anyway.

"Could you please send these to *The Virginia*? It leaves at eleven o'clock," Adelida asked Miss Frannie. She'd take care of Rueben's last, little, smart aleck remark later, and they'd just see who could win the argument.

"Yes, ma'am, Mrs. Hamilton. They will be waiting in your stateroom when you arrive," Miss Frannie said.

"Thank you so much," Adelida shook hands with the woman. "Rueben, are you ready? I hope you weren't too bored."

"Not at all. The newspaper kept me occupied," he said.

The new spy was sitting on a wooden bench in front of the store when they left. He followed them.

Charleston's finest tailors netted Rueben two suits, sev-eral collars and white shirts, and an assortment of short-alls. The proprietor directed them to a boot shop several blocks away for new footwear. The spy kept so close they could almost smell the man.

"He's not nearly as sly as the last one. If it hadn't been for that first one's cigars he might very well have gotten away with it," Rueben whispered.

"Well, I'm tired of this, *mon ami*," she said.

"*Mon ami* is better than sugar," he mumbled. "That's something you call a little baby before it's old enough to walk."

"It's what you call anyone who is sweet and kind, and either one can be said in sarcasm, which that was," she retorted, unlooping her arm from his and walking back to the spy who had stopped at a confectionery window.

"Hello," she said brightly. "Are you from around Charleston? My husband and I are on the ship *The Virginia*, and we've only got a little while to see the sights. I'm meeting his mother for the very first time and I'd like to take them something as a gift. My mama in Louisiana said a woman never goes to her in-laws without a gift to sweeten the mother-in-law. So could you tell me, if you are from Charleston, is this a good place to buy candies? I'm sure that would be an appropriate gift, but I'm not so sure about these Yankees and their likes and dislikes. It's going to be such a change from the bayou where I was raised."

"I'm not from here, but I would say candy would be fine," the man said, his pock marked face and bad teeth not matching the expensive suit he wore.

"Well, I do thank you. Where are you from?" she asked bluntly.

"New York. I'm on that same ship. Noticed you this morning at breakfast," he said.

"Would you mind just stepping in the store with me for a minute and helping me choose a few of these delicious looking sweets? No, of course you wouldn't," she had him by the arm and inside the store before he could utter a word.

"But your husband?" The man actually reddened around the ears.

"Oh, he knows nothing of sweets, and he wanted to buy his mother a new frying pan as a gift, but she would probably hit me on the head with it. Since he's being stubborn and will not help me, I told him I would ask a local person for assistance. I'm having sweets for her even if he thinks it's the wrong present. Now what do you think of these?" She pointed toward the end of the candy counter, far away from the window.

"They look fine to me," he said, his eyes darting around like he was the cornered rabbit in a store filled with hungry alligators.

"Then we shall have a pound of those," Adelida said. "And two extra pieces to pay this nice man for being kind enough to help me."

The whole transaction took less than five minutes and when Adelida and the spy were back on the street, Rueben was walking back toward them, a worried look on his face.

"Whatever took so long?" he said.

"Ah, so many sweets to choose from," she said. "My thanks to you, sir. Now let's go see some more of this town before we have to get back on the ship. Would you like to join us?"

"No, thank you. I have somewhere . . ." he stammered.

"Thank you for helping my wife. She was determined to buy candy," Rueben said. Sweet Jesus, what could Adelida be thinking? The man looked like a killer for sure, one who'd think nothing of wringing her neck right there in the candy store.

"You are welcome," he said, waiting in front of the store until they were a few feet ahead of him before he followed again.

"Don't you ever pull a stunt like that again," Rueben hissed between clenched teeth. "That man is dangerous. He'll kill you in a minute."

"Not until he knows for sure where *it* is. *Bon Dieu*, what is that?" she asked.

"Looks to be a rather large hotel. I mean it. Don't play games with him. Maybe he'll give up and stay in Charleston," Rueben said.

"But it's pink," she said.

"Yes, it is. Never seen a pink hotel before?" he asked, looking over his shoulder. The spy was still there.

"I don't think so. It's so big and so pink. I can't believe any woman on the face of the earth could talk her husband into staying in a pink hotel. It would rob him of his masculinity. After a night in that place he might want to wear lace-trimmed drawers," she teased.

Rueben threw back his head and roared, laughter erasing some of the tension. "Do you always speak your mind so openly?" he asked, wiping his eyes with the handkerchief he pulled from his pocket.

"Yes, I most certainly do. That's why I'm still not . . . you know," she glanced backwards. "There's not a man in the bayou who'd want a woman who spoke her mind. They want little simpering, sweet women who bend to their every beck and call and never open their mouth to express an opinion. But I wasn't raised that way. My mama said what she thought. Didn't mince her words one bit. Maybe we should go in that pink hotel and pretend we're getting a room. I bet that spy wouldn't enter the front doors. Can you see him in lace-trimmed underwear and a fancy little nightcap on his head?"

Rueben laughed again and leaned down to whisper in her ear. "Is that the kind of man that appeals to you? Is that what you want when you are a rich woman and you go looking for a husband? Or when you try to outrun one of the many men who try to catch you for your money?"

They walked several minutes in silence while she thought about the questions. She stopped in front of a furniture store and kissed Rueben on the cheek, whispering her answer, "I want a man who is kind and who can laugh like you do. I want him to be a real man, not a whimpering fool. And let me tell you, those who are chasing after me with nothing more than dollar signs in their eyes better get ready for a race."

So, she thought he was kind and liked the way he laughed, did she? That, added to the fact she'd once called him handsome, put a little more spring in his step.

"And what will you be looking for in a Yankee wife when I give your ring back at the end of our journey somewhere near your Love's Valley?" she asked very softly.

"Someone who will be content to live in my valley during the bad times and the good times, who'll raise up a family of children with me and sit on the porch when we are old and gray and watch our grandchildren play on the green grass in the summer time, and who'll go outside and have snowball fights with our children and who'll fit in with the rest of my family," he said, hoping the spy took their conversation as sweet endearments passed back and forth between a newlywed couple very much in love.

That ended the idea that she might and could fall for Rueben Hamilton. They'd had so much fun today outwitting the spy, shopping, talking openly about things. They were really becoming good friends, building a foundation that something else might be founded upon.

But to fit in with his family? Simply not possible.

Chapter Twelve

Being in love with Henry Rueben Hamilton didn't sweeten Adelida Broussau's temperament one bit. When she realized that 'like' didn't begin to cover the feelings she had for the man, it was as if she'd drank the juice from a whole crock of dill pickles. Now what was she supposed to do? She was a Southern woman, mayhap a rich one if Reed's ship found all that treasure, but even all that money couldn't change that she was from the bayou. If she took all the jewels in those trunks and draped them all over a nice, clean, little piglet, it wouldn't change the fact that under the jewels was nothing more than a plain old hog. Being rich didn't suddenly change Adelida into someone Rueben could or would love. Not that she would have changed one bit for him anyway. Rueben simply wasn't the right man, because when the right one came along, he'd take her exactly as she stood and not change a thing.

But she did love him and it would have to be undone. Out of sight, out of mind the old women used to say on the

141

Bayou Penchant. She'd make that adage her motto, she decided as she flipped through the pages of a month old newspaper and did her best to ignore Rueben sitting right beside her. After she had seen his mountains and felt the cool mountain breezes on her face, she just might go on back home to the bayou. She might buy a sugar plantation and invite all her bayou relatives to help her raise the sugar. Until then she would fight this business of being in love with Rueben Hamilton every step of the way, and when Adelida Broussau engaged in a battle, she did not lose.

Rueben stretched his long, lanky frame out in the chaise lounge on the ship's deck and read an article in an old Savannah newspaper. Some naturalist named John Muir had got a burr in his long johns and had taken it upon himself to walk all the way from Louisville, Kentucky, to the tip of mainland Florida. He'd come through Savannah a few weeks earlier and stayed at the Bonaventure plantation there. The article was all about his adventure. People were tired of hearing war stories and sick to death of articles about the Texas land wars, the Reconstruction, the riots. So Mr. Muir had picked a good time to make his sojourn and tell of what he'd seen in all those miles.

So why, if they were so intrigued with something like that, was it such a crime for a man of Northern birth and persuasion in the war to fall for a woman who'd been raised in the bayou country of Louisiana? If everyone was ready to put the war behind them, then why did it matter who a man chose for a wife?

Whoa, he braked at that train of thought. *She'd clash with every woman in your family, all except that Texan that Monroe dragged home. You ready to make that kind of choice?* He laid the paper aside and stole a glance over at her.

"Looks like we're docking. Shall we check out the beach?" he asked.

"I don't know why. An hour is barely enough to warrant getting off the boat," she said testily.

"It beats another three days on the ship," Rueben shot back. "At least we'll have a nice stroll. Who knows, maybe our spy will even join us."

"I'm sorry, Rueben. I'm so tired of all this play acting. But if he's going to follow us, shall we give him a merry chase?"

"An apology from the Cajun. I'm stunned."

"You'd better be. You probably won't ever hear another one. Now what do you have in mind?"

Rueben grinned, that slight dimple in his chin deepening. "I've got a wonderful idea. It's childish, but I'm tired of all this too. Let's go get some paper and leave him a map."

His smile wiped away the sour mood and the two of them were cohorts again. She even kept her hand in his when he helped her from the chaise lounge. "What are we going to do?" she whispered.

"Drop a letter in the sand about two minutes before we are to board the ship again. If he's really a spy and not just some fellow enamored with you, he'll be all excited that he's found something concrete to tell his captain about the island. If you would have let me call the man out for a duel all this wouldn't be happening," Rueben said.

"Then you would either be dead, and I'm not doubting your ability to draw faster or sword fight better than that horrible man, or you would be in jail for murder. Neither of which would gain me any points with your family. And what is this letter going to say?"

Rueben loved it when her eyes glistened in excitement. He wanted nothing more than to be the one who kept that glow alive in those dark brown eyes, but she'd never fall for a dull man like the middle Hamilton son. Adelida deserved a man who'd take her to exotic places and show her the world.

"I know. I know," she grabbed a piece of paper and began to write. When she finished she handed it to him.

Dear Spy, We know you are following us. We know you are interested in the treasure we left on the island. Please tell your benefactor that the armoire is filled with the most wonderful surprises. I left two pairs of lady's unmentionables in the first drawer. Pure silk and big enough to make a mast for a small schooner. Then there was a lovely hat in the top shelf. I'm sure it could be repaired and wearable with very little effort. There is a whole crop of lovely oranges going to waste on the lower end of the island. And if you dig real hard you can find some of the best clams in the whole world. There is also enough seaweed to make a lovely clam bake. Other than that, if you chartered a ship and went to the island, provided you could find it, I am sure at this time that you would find absolutely nothing more. So why are you continuing to follow us?

Rueben chuckled at the end. "That'll make him really mad, to know we know he's a spy."

"Good, I've been mad that he's following us," Adelida said. "Here, let's make him even more angry."

Rueben handed the piece of paper back to her and watched as she turned it over and drew a map of the whole island. It was a bit longer than wide, with trees with round balls on the one end that were oranges. With her inaccurate eye for dimension, though, the oranges would have been only slightly smaller than full grown watermelons. Near the beach, she drew the cistern and labeled it as such, then drew a big oblong shape and wrote *armoire* on the picture. Right above that she made a huge X with a skull and crossbones beside it.

"A map?" Rueben asked.

"Sure, and I'll bet you that when we dock at Hampton, Virginia, tomorrow night he can't wait to get off this ship and go show it to whoever has hired him. I bet you he can't even read," Adelida said.

Rueben folded the note carefully and shoved it deep into his trouser pocket. Along with more than a hundred other passengers, they left the ship for a stroll on the sandy beach. Mail would be unloaded and reloaded while they were docked. Fresh water would be taken on and cargo put off, but the passengers could have cared less. They just wanted a while away from the continual boredom of travel.

Adelida took off her shoes and stockings on the beach, wiggling her toes in the soft, warm sand. "Ah," she said, "home at last. I didn't think I'd ever miss the feel of dirt on my feet, but I do." She stuffed her stockings inside the shoes and tied the laces together, draping them around her neck like an expensive scarf.

"Do you really intend to take your walk barefoot?" he asked, taken back at such a brazen act. No self-respecting woman would ever let her ankles and toes show like that.

"Yes, I do," she nodded. "Does that embarrass you?"

"Of course it does darlin'," a little gray-haired lady giggled right behind her. "Men folks are much more squeamish about doing something against society than women. If I could get up once I sat down to take off my shoes, I'd join you. I was raised up on the beaches in Maine and we'd run barefoot in the sand all summer."

"I'll help you," Adelida offered.

"Oh no, you won't," the lady shook her head, all three chins wiggling in the effort. "You and that handsome husband of yours are going to take a long walk and whisper sweet talk in each other's ears. Go be romantic."

"We'll do it," Adelida nodded.

"We will?" Rueben asked, when they'd gotten out of hearing distance of the sweet little lady.

"Will what?" Adelida asked, her thoughts on how delightful the sand felt when she buried her toes in it as she walked.

"Be romantic?" Rueben asked.

"Why would we be?" Adelida looked up into his green eyes.

"You told that lady that we'd be romantic," he reminded her.

"I was just saying what she wanted to hear. I'm beginning to think we'd both make almighty fine actors on the stage. Ever since you got your memory back, we've had to pretend the whole time to protect our interests. I think I've got this wife thing down."

"Oh, and what is it a wife does besides whine and argue and fuss about every little thing?"

"She puts up with a husband who ignores her and stares at other women. She listens to him snore. She digs more clams than he does, but doesn't eat as many when they're cooked."

"Then I suppose we do have the act down."

"How far is it to the mountains where you live now?" she asked, stopping to pick up a conch shell, pink on the inside and bigger than Rueben's fist.

"Five days, but you could stay in Baltimore. I'll set you

up in a nice hotel and talk to the bank of your choice about the money," he said.

"No, thank you," she shook her head. "I'm going to your mountains. You said there was a town nearby."

"You don't trust me," he snapped.

"I would not wholly trust an angel with big, white, feathery wings and a golden halo standing before me playing a harp, Mr. Hamilton. Money makes rascals of the most trustworthy men. I'll just stay right beside you until my half is securely in my name with no strings attached. I don't intend to ever walk into a bank again and have a teller tell me some man has taken my fortune and that I don't even have enough money to buy a biscuit."

"How do you plan on doing just that?"

"What, stay beside you? Or having money with no strings attached?"

"Adelida, Shirleysburg is a small town. Everyone knows everyone's business. For a small fortune to come through the bank for me, that's one thing. The Hamiltons deal in big numbers with all the businesses we take care of. But when a fortune the size of what we'll have arrives in your name, it won't be a week until you'll have more notoriety than you can handle," he said.

"I can handle anything," she told him bluntly. "When we get to Shirleysburg I want a hotel room. They do have a hotel there, don't they?"

"Yes. And when I take you in the front door and register you, you'll immediately have a reputation as wicked as those women in the brothel in Charleston. You will be traveling with a man who is not your husband. You'll have no chaperone," he reminded her.

"Then maybe I'll build a house, a big one, and paint it pink," she said.

"You wouldn't," he gritted his teeth.

"I might," she told him.

"No one is following us." He tried to change the subject.

"Don't you do that, Rueben. Don't run from a conversation because you're losing ground," she stopped and accentuated every word by poking her finger in his chest.

"There's no use conversing with a stubborn mule," he grabbed her hand and held it tightly.

"Oh, are you calling me a mule? That would be the pot calling the kettle black for sure. You are one bull-headed man." Her eyes narrowed as she pried her hand away from his.

Something glittered up on the hill. She watched carefully and saw it again. "Rueben, let's not fight. We're supposed to be romantic like the lady said, not battling with each other," she walked into his chest and wrapped her arms around his neck.

"What in the devil are you doing?" He tried to unwrap her arms, but in the midst of it looked down into her face. Brown eyes, a moment ago fuming, now looked soft and lazy. Lips that had been uttering meanness now begged for a passionate kiss. Against those two, Rueben had no defenses. He leaned forward and claimed her full sensuous mouth. The kiss, soft at first, deepened into a searching of two souls desperate to find their mates.

"Well, that was a very convincing act," she continued to hug him even when the kiss had finished. "The spy is up on that hill with a glass watching our every move. If you look over my left shoulder you can see it twinkling in the trees."

"So we're acting again?"

"Of course, you didn't think I'd kiss you for any other reason, did you? And you wouldn't waste such passion on me if we weren't acting, now would you, Rueben?"

"No ma'am," he said, pushing her back and retrieving

the folded paper from his pocket. "I suppose it's time to drop our map."

"Yes, it is, and then you can take my hand in yours and we'll pretend to be in love all the way back to the ship."

Rueben fumbled in the pocket of his jacket and brought out a handkerchief, letting the note flutter to the ground and ignoring it. Using his fist, he tilted Adelida's chin back and dabbed at her eyes. "That should make our spy think you merely have something in your eye. The note is on the ground. Don't look down or back once we start walking."

"Very clever, my husband," she smiled up at him as he wiped the imaginary sand from her eyes.

They watched from the deck as the spy hurried back on board. They both wondered how much of what had gone on had truly been acting and what had been real. What had been fun and what had been a ploy to outwit a spy?

"Let's go to our room. I'm sleepy," she finally whispered. She needed some time to think about the kiss that still warmed her lips and heated her heart to the boiling point.

"Me too," he faked a yawn. Five days and they'd be in Shirleysburg. A day or two past that and she'd be gone. The future looked bleak.

Chapter Thirteen

Adelida dreamed of sitting on the banks of a creek, dangling her feet in the icy cold, clear water where minnows nibbled playfully on the ends of her toes. Rueben baited a fishing hook at the end of the line attached to a cane pole and threw it out into the water. The glow of a freshly risen sun bathed them both in a brand new day.

Then suddenly she was kicking and flailing, trying to get her breath, to push a big, rough hand away from her mouth and nose.

"Hush," a harsh voice said. "Make a sound and your husband over there gets his throat cut like a pig. Do you understand me, woman?"

Her eyes snapped open to find Rueben tied to a chair, a gag in his mouth and a nasty cut on his forehead. She hoped the wicked idiot hadn't sent Rueben back into that amnesiac state where he didn't know who he was again. She jerked her head around to really look at the man whose vile-smelling hand covered her mouth.

"Do you understand? Do you want to see your husband die?" he asked again, his foul breath nauseating her.

"I understand," she mumbled.

"Good." He let go of her mouth and twisted an arm up around her back, leading her to the bed where he tossed her like a bag of chicken feed into the middle of it. "Now, you'll sit right there. I'm going to lay this blade right gentle like on his throat and ask you questions. First time I think you're a lyin' to me, I'll shave his Adam's apple off so fast you'll wonder if it was ever there. Are you listenin' to me?"

She nodded, afraid to trust her voice again. The blade was honed to a fine, sharp finish that glowed in the moonlight.

"I'm not a fool, but you got to think I am with that little map you dropped. Do you think I can't read? I can read, lady, and you were making fun of me. You did find something on that island or you wouldn't have made up something so silly to protect it. If you hadn't, you wouldn't even know I had been watching you."

Rueben sat very still and hoped Adelida didn't play games.

Adelida stared at the man, hatred pouring out of her eyes. "We got tired of you following us. You're not a very good spy," she said finally. He'd kill them both, but she wasn't going to die without a fight.

"I might not be a good spy, but I'm very good at murder," he flicked the end of the knife just enough to bring a bubble of blood to Rueben's throat. "I hear tell you two was washed up on an island and that you was askin' the captain questions about where it was, that you pulled a knife on him during a dance. That right?"

Adelida hesitated, and he fingered the knife as if it were the soft skin of a woman's bare arm. She had no doubt he'd kill Rueben in an instant. Was all the money worth watching Rueben die and then suffering through whatever the evil man would do to her?

"What do you want to know?" she asked, bringing his attention back to her.

"I want to know if you found something like money or jewels out there on that island where you found the knife. It was a fancy thing like they used a hun'urd years ago, Captain Gilford said. The captain knows them things. He thinks you're plannin' to go back out there to get the treasure or send someone after it."

Adelida figured it had been four days since they'd left Savannah and it had taken five days to get there from the island. Reed's ships should be almost to the island by now unless bad weather had slowed them down. One swift telegram from the spy and the adulterous captain could have a ship in the water to beat Reed's ships. Could Reed's company make it to the island before the wicked captain's?

It was a judgment call at best.

"What is it I can tell you?"

"I want to know the truth, woman. The pure truth. What did you see out there on that island that made your man here ask where it was? What made you act the way you did to raise up the captain's hackles? He ain't never wrong about his feelings. He knowed you was up to something. He said he could smell the excitement in you."

"Well, we got there and we saw a cistern right in the middle of the island," she said. "It had a bamboo tube running down one leg of the cistern into the ground so my husband—why should I answer you? You're going to kill us anyway," she started to stand up.

"Sit down or he dies," the man growled.

She sat down.

"Go on and tell me about the cistern. What was in it?"

"The bamboo tube was just a trick," she lied. She'd tell

him what he wanted to hear, but his men would work for the treasure if they reached the island first.

"Go on," he said.

"There is a top on the cistern. No way it could catch rain water. Rueben crawled up there and took off one of the boards. There's jewels and lots and lots of gold inside it," she said.

"Why didn't you tell the captain? He'd a shared it with you. Now you ain't goin' to have nothing because I'm goin' to send a telegram and tell him to go right back there and find all that treasure," the man stepped away from Rueben.

"Tell him to be careful. The reason we didn't try to bring it out ourselves is because of those snakes. Big old poisonous snakes with orange circles around their bellies," Adelida shrugged. "We were able to grab a hand full of gold and a couple of necklaces, but that's all. Ain't no way we'd fight those snakes even for that treasure. You can have it."

"You are both fools. Snakes can be killed," he said.

"I suppose, but we didn't have knives or guns like you'll have when you go back there. Besides there was two skeletons that convinced us the snakes were evil. Some things ain't worth the trouble it causes."

Rueben shook his head and tried to speak. If the man would just ungag him, he'd tell him the real truth, anything to protect Adelida's pretty white skin. The minute they went to the island and found nothing but water in that cistern, they'd come all the way back to Shirleysburg and kill her for the lies she'd told. No man, especially a hired killer, wants to be made a fool of.

"Stop it or I'll slice you up just because you're such a Yankee dandy," the man told him.

"Leave him alone. You got what you wanted," Adelida yelled.

"Yep, I did," he grinned. "All but one little thing. I had a mind to take you with me to be mine for a while. You ain't really his. The captain said so. Said he could tell you weren't married. But the captain, he said I can't have you."

Rueben didn't know he was holding his breath until it escaped him in a whoosh.

"Had you worried there, didn't I?" The man chuckled at Rueben. "Guess you ain't finished with the goods just yet. But I don't want to worry none about you comin' after me so I'm going to tie you up too. I'm goin' to put my knife right here between my teeth and show you a little trick." Before Adelida could blink he'd spit the knife out into his hands and had it planted firmly on her throat. "That's how quick I can make a dead woman out of you. It won't be botherin' me a bit to do it, neither, so you be a nice little lady and be right still. Now lay back on that bed, on your back."

She did what she was told, terror clinching her soul, anger filling her breast. Once he tied her up, she'd be at his mercy with Rueben watching, his eyes almost shooting fire at the man. He would protect her if he could and that notion brought a soft, warm feeling to the depths of her heart. The spy used rope to tie her legs to the footboard and her hands to the headboard, spread out in such a fashion that embarrassed her nigh unto death. Then he pulled a filthy handkerchief from his pocket and gagged her.

"Right tempting to sample the goods and then slit your pretty white throat," he licked his lips. "But the captain said not to kill you unless it was needful." He pulled the gag from her mouth. "How'd you know I was follerin' you? You didn't know the man you took to dinner was a spy too, did you? He listened to every fight you two had. Me, I think the captain is wrong about the marriage. I think you probably are married. You sure do argue and fuss like you done been married a hun'erd years ruther than a few weeks."

Adelida glared at him.

"Tell me how you knowed I was a spy and I'll leave that gag off'n you. Everyone will be getting off the ship in a few minutes, so it won't be doin' you no good to be screamin'." He ran the flat edge of the knife down her neck.

She fought the bile back into her stomach. She wouldn't give him the satisfaction of seeing her retch. "Next time don't use a spy glass. We saw the reflection."

"Nope, I ain't buyin' that," he said. "You already had that cutesy little note made up so you knowed I was fol-lerin' you fore that."

"Okay. We figured it out in Charleston when every-where we looked you were there," she said.

"Couldn't let you out of my sight," he chuckled. "Guess I'll have to remember that next time to be more careful."

"Why didn't the captain just go back to the island or send someone and find the treasure himself rather than chasing after us?"

Rueben would have gladly wrung her pretty neck for that question. The man was already halfway to the door when she asked.

"He did. Soon as he could he sent off a telegram to his buddies and they went right away. Dug all over the south end of the island. Figured that's where you would've hid it if you found anything. You sure wouldn't have put it right there where they found you. They smashed that big old closet thing to pieces looking for secret places. Didn't find a thing. Never thought to look in the cistern, though. Just figured it to be what it was. Now they'll know to look there. Reckon they'll be hittin' that soon now."

"And what if the people who hid it has already gone and gotten it?"

Rueben swore if he ever got loose he was going to strangle her until her pretty brown eyes popped out and her face turned the color of the summer sky.

"Them pirates that hid that is long since dead or they would have already been back. The captain is a smart man. He knows about those things." He shut the door quietly.

Rueben and Adelida heard a click as he turned the key, leaving them in a locked room. Rueben exhaled as best he could around the gag.

"Don't you look at me like that," Adelida hissed at him. "I know you're angry because I asked him those questions, but I wanted to know if he was going to come back and kill us, even in Love's Valley."

"You are not going to Love's Valley, lady," he tried to say but only a mumble escaped the gag.

"Don't try to talk," she told him. "Just be very quiet and sit still. I can get us out of this."

Oh, sure, and I can jump right up and dance a little jig for you. Would you like a waltz or how about a fast little reel? He glared at her.

"When I was little, I got it in my head that I was going to be a magic person. I practiced little tricks with cards, then decided I was going to practice real magic. Besides I've got a trick thumb," she talked as she carefully turned her wrist until she had the thumb in the right position.

Magic! It will take more than magic for you to get out of those ropes. It would take a pure miracle from heaven.

However, with what looked like the mere flick of a finger or two from where he sat, she slipped her small hand through the rope.

Well, I'll be hung for a rebel! He figured she'd slip her other hand from the ropes as easily, but she didn't.

"Don't look so disgusted," she said. "I've only got one thumb that's double jointed and can move like that. The rest will have to come slowly as I work the knots loose. And that fool sure knew how to tie some good knots. What I'd give to have my knife."

It took her the better part of an hour to free her left hand. The sun was rising by the time she'd sat up and worked through the knots on her ankles. What she'd said in Cajun French would've scorched the devil's ears, and Rueben was glad he didn't understand more than a few words of the tirade.

"I hope there is a big poisonous snake in the cistern. A water moccasin that hasn't had its fangs in flesh in twenty years. Big as your arm and hungry as a 'gater that hasn't eaten in weeks," she mumbled, as she finally untied the last rope.

She rubbed feeling back into her ankles so she wouldn't fall flat on her face when she stood on her feet. When they'd stopped tingling, she tested them on the floor and eased her way over to Rueben, whose eyes were full of rage. Even with the nick on his throat and the head wound encrusted in dried blood, he was still the most handsome man she'd ever seen.

She untied the gag and jerked it free first.

"You could have been killed if he'd figured out you were lying." Rueben tried to yell, but his voice was gone and his mouth dry from the gag.

"But he didn't. They might find the treasure, but they're going to work for it," she dug in the trunk for the jewel-bedecked knife. "Now, be still and let me cut you loose. I'm just thankful he didn't hit you hard enough to erase your memory again."

"I know who I am and who you are," he said between clenched teeth, the very idea of a woman being the one to set them free grating on his nerves as much as being rendered helpless by that sorry scoundrel in the first place.

"Good, and I suppose you've already figured out that we've only got a little while before the ship docks. We've got to get to the captain and tell him the man is a spy and he threatened to kill us," she said, sitting on the floor behind him and rubbing his chafed wrists to bring back circulation.

"Yes, I did," he said hoarsely. He couldn't wait to find the captain and have the man arrested. With him in jail, Reed's men would have a better chance of sneaking in and out of the island. It would be a race to the treasure now, and Rueben was not going to lose.

"Hey, don't be mad at me. I didn't tell that spy to sneak in here. Be mad at him, not at me," she said, cutting through the ropes around his ankles.

"I am mad at you. You could have been killed if he'd had any idea you were lying. Men are crazy when it comes to money, Adelida," he wanted to take her in his arms and hold her tight against his chest.

"And women are supposed to be little simpering mouses who'll tell anything to spare them or their loved ones hurt. I played on that and his arrogance," she poured a basin of water from the pitcher on the washstand, wet a cloth and began dabbing away the blood from his forehead.

Sensations, tense and real, shot through his body when she held his chin in her small hand to keep him steady.

"Let me clean you up while you wait for your legs to get

some feeling back or you'll wind up on the floor. He tied you even tighter than me. I bet your feet feel like they've got knives sticking in them right about now, huh, *cher*?"

Rueben nodded. "We don't have time to waste. I can walk."

Rueben stumbled stiffly toward the armoire to get his clothes.

"Hurry up," he told Adelida, who'd disappeared behind the screen.

"I am hurrying," she snapped. "But we've got to figure out how to get out of here, too, Rueben. We're locked in and he took the key. Makes me wonder how he got inside in the first place. Guess he picked the lock."

"Just stop talking and hurry. You opened the armoire with a hairpin. Do you think you've got any more magic up your sleeve?"

"Of course," she said.

Rueben shoved his legs into trousers and buttoned a shirt across his broad chest. He'd been ready to tell her how much he loved her when he was tied up, but now that they were free, all he wanted to do was scream at her. She might as well put the gag back in his mouth. He couldn't say a word.

Adelida stepped from behind the dressing screen and ran smack into Rueben's chest. He encircled her in his arms, pulling her into the embrace. The soft rhythmic thud of his heart was balm to her own still anxious, quivering insides. That he didn't return the love she felt for him didn't matter. The only thing that did was that she found comfort and peace in the circle of his arms.

He cleared his dry throat and looked down into those mesmerizing deep eyes. "I suppose we'd better pick that lock."

She nodded, unable to speak, wanting to touch her lips to his. Instead, she reached up and pulled a pin from her hair.

She swore. "I can't make it open."

"What do you mean, you can't open it?"

"I just can't, Rueben. Do you think you can shove me through that port hole?" She threw the hairpin on the floor and eyed the window.

"No, as tiny as you are, you'd never fit through there," he said. "Just stand back, Adelida. I know how to get that door open."

"But . . ." she started to argue.

He ran at it, shoving his shoulder into the impact. The wood splintered and held. The second time more wood broke loose. The third time the lock broke and the door swung open. They both rushed out to find the captain of the ship.

Moments later, they found him.

"But we have already docked and the man you are talking about was the first one off the ship," he told them.

"He threatened to kill us," Rueben said again.

"Then take your story to the sheriff. It's out of my hands now," the captain told them.

The sheriff listened to their story and sent a deputy to the telegraph office. In a few minutes he reported back that a man of that description had indeed sent a telegram earlier, but several people had sent messages since so the dispatcher couldn't remember what the telegram was about.

"If we see someone like that, we'll bring him in for questioning," the sheriff told Rueben. "But at this point, it will simply be his word against yours. He can say that you have been following him and this is all a ploy."

"But it's not. We were shipwrecked on the island," Adelida started to explain again.

"It doesn't matter," Rueben told her. "We have nothing to prove our story. Thank you for your efforts, Sheriff."

"Sorry I couldn't be more help," he said.

"I've got to send a gram to Reed," Rueben said when they were outside. "If he can get a message to our men, they need to know the danger they could be in."

Four men anchored a small ship near the island. Two of them stayed with the ship. Two were lowered down in lifeboats and rowed out to the shore. They dragged their boats up on the beach and went straight for the cistern. They dug in the sand and finally found the door to the cellar.

"We found it," one said.

"Let's load it up and get out of here. Reed said there were skeletons down here, and I've got a funny feeling about being around the dead," the other one said.

"Me too, man, but look at this stuff," he wandered from one small chest to the other. Three filled with money. Three with jewels. "Think we can get it all with one load?"

"They're pretty heavy. Let's make it in two trips. It'll take us both to carry each one to the shore."

They tested the weight of two in each rowboat and figured they could get away with that much. It took an hour to get out to the ship and back again. They were near the cistern when they looked out to sea on the other side of the island and saw another ship.

"Looks like we got company, Alford," one said.

"Looks like it, Joe," the other nodded.

"Think we can get the other two out and get away before they see us?" Alford asked.

"Maybe. Reed said there were spies. I've got an idea. Might save Reed's brother some heartache. We'll divide the money and jewels and leave one chest behind. They'll find something and think that's the whole hog," Joe said.

Alford nodded in agreement.

"I'd planned on giving those two fellers in the other room a decent burial," Joe said, when they had the chest closed and ready to haul up the steps. "Guess it's too late now."

"For sure," Alford stared at the two skeletons.

"Okay then, let's get this last chest out of here. We'll make it easy for those other men to find what we're leaving them. Even leave them a few clues," Alford picked up a ruby bracelet from the open chest they left in the cellar. He tossed the bracelet on the ground beside the cistern and kicked a few inches of dirt back over the cellar door, leaving enough wood showing on the bottom corner that they'd find it easily enough.

The second set of men, four of them, didn't even see the other ship as it disappeared between the islands. They crawled carefully up to the top of the cistern, expecting snakes to come slithering out at any moment. Surprise was written on their faces when they found nothing in the cistern but rainwater.

"That witch lied," one screamed.

"But look," another one asked, looking down and seeing the bracelet. "She might have lied but we'll find the treasure. Look, she's dropped a piece. She ain't as smart as she thought she was, now is she? We'll find it anyway."

They scampered down like ants and began digging in the sand where the bracelet had been tossed. It took them more than an hour, but they did find the cellar door and the chest.

"Well, would you look at this? Captain Gilford was

right all along. Bet they took a few pieces out along with that knife, but they had to leave all the rest of it behind. And we got to it before they could send somebody back. Now ain't that too bad," one laughed.

"Let's see if there's any more," one of the others threw open the door to the room where the skeletons were.

"Good god, let's get out of here," he jumped back.

They didn't waste any time gathering their booty and getting away from the dead.

Chapter Fourteen

Adelida paced from one end of the hotel room to the other. She'd spent weeks with Rueben only a few feet away from her and wishing for a room of her own. Now she had just that and didn't want it. Pouring rain beat against the closed window. The room was muggy and the night every bit as hot as it would have been in New Orleans. She'd stripped down to her drawers and camisole, but it wouldn't matter if she wore nothing; she'd still be too warm and the downpour would keep the window shut all night, so there would be no relief from a cool night breeze.

Her pacing path looped around the big bed with its headboard shoved against the wall to the washstand with a mirror above it, to the door and back to the bed. She was determined she'd settle the angst in her heart or else wear out the floorboards in the hotel. Different scenarios played in her mind. Rueben would laugh at her if she told him she'd fallen in love with him. Rueben would tell her there was no way she was going with him another mile. Rueben would tell her she was crazy as a snake-bitten 'gater for ever thinking he could love a bayou woman. He was a Hamilton. They married their own kind.

Finally she gave up creating scenes and threw herself on the bed—a fine feather bed with crisp, ironed sheets. Rueben had made sure they were booked into the finest hotel he could find and he'd already purchased rail tickets at the Mount Clare Train Station to take them from Baltimore to a place in Martinsburg, Virginia. She'd never been on a train, but her brothers had talked about it in their letters. Perhaps that was the reason she was so restless, not out of fear but from sheer excitement. The train would take them as far as it could and then that thrill would be over. Soon it would all be over. She'd see the mountains for herself and it would be finished. There'd be nothing left but to reverse the trip and go home, or else find Evangeline and play poker on the steamships. Fishing or poker. She'd didn't have to make the decision right away, though. Tomorrow night, Rueben had said, they'd be in another hotel room and from there the trip would be made by stage coach. Who would've thought that Adelida Broussau, the fisherman's daughter from the Bayou Penchant, would have had so many adventures?

"Who would have thought she'd lose her heart to a low-down Yankee?" she mumbled.

She flipped from one side to the other, beat her pillow into submission, then shut her eyes, but sleep wouldn't come. After an hour she arose, threw on a robe, buttoned it all the way down the front and peeked out the door. The coast was clear, and if she didn't get a breath of fresh air, she was going to suffocate.

She padded barefoot down the wide, highly-polished oak staircase and out the front door to the swing she'd seen earlier. Rain and rose-scented breezes greeted her like a familiar, old friend. Located in the depths of a corner and protected by rose-covered lattice work, the swing was still dry. She sat down, pulled her knees up to her chin and wrapped her arms around them.

Life was now good. Adelida Broussau wasn't made to live in a cooped-up house forever and this evening had proven it to her. She was a swamp rat with a need to sleep under the stars on the deck of a fishing boat. "But I could live in a house with a foundation if I could leave the window cracked," she mumbled.

Fresh air and the lull of the swing moving as gentle as the summer breeze reminded her of the bayou and the boat. Finally she fell asleep and dreamed of a picnic, the last one before the war when she and her brothers joined the rest of the Broussaus and the Boudreaxs for a family reunion. There was laughing and feasting, babies to kiss, brides to congratulate, mood-lifting Cajun music, and dancing. Right in the middle of it, Rueben appeared on a huge chestnut horse yelling that the war had come and the South was going to lose.

She'd been dancing a fast reel, and he swooped her up into his arms. She felt herself leave the ground, and in spite of the fact her brothers and cousins were screaming that she could not go away with a Yankee, she kept her eyes closed. The dream couldn't end, not until she and Rueben had a real talk. She tucked her chin deeper into her chest to avoid the bristles of a day old beard and the sourness of his breath.

"So you waited for me, did you? Does that mean I'm forgiven?" A husky voice whispered in her ear.

It was not Rueben Hamilton's voice. She stiffened and her eyes popped open wide just as the man reached the top of the stairs. She began to fight him, beating at his chest and face with her fists and screaming in Cajun French loud enough to wake the whole town of Baltimore.

"Stop fightin' me. You waited for me," he kept saying,

tightening his drunken hold on her and trying to hush her protests with unwanted kisses.

"What is going on?" A door swung open and a small dark-haired woman stormed out into the hall. "You sorry piece of trash," she screamed at Adelida and the man. "Daddy said I shouldn't marry a drinking man and he was right."

Rueben had been sleeping soundly, when he heard Adelida's screams. The melee that greeted him when he opened the door was enough to stagger a stone cold sober man. Adelida was hollering in Cajun. Another woman about the same size as Adelida was yelling in a Texas drawl. Eyes peered out of every doorway in the hall.

The confused man finally opened his arms and tossed Adelida to the floor like a bag of chicken feed. "I thought she was you. I thought you'd waited up for me and I was carrying you back up to the room."

"Sure you did," the woman slapped him. "You snuck out to drink again and found yourself a woman. Thought you'd sneak into her room, didn't you?"

"He did not," Adelida jumped to her feet and went nose-to-nose with the lady. "I couldn't sleep so I went down to get a breath of fresh air and fell asleep on the swing. I don't know if he really thought I was you or what, but you might listen to his story."

"I've listened to too many of his stories already," she said. "But we're making a spectacle of ourselves, Alvin. We can take our fight in our own room."

"I suppose we can," he said in a tense voice, suddenly more sober than he'd been in a long time. How could he have mistaken that woman for his wife?

"Adelida?" Rueben asked.

She jerked her head around toward the voice. "It's the truth. I fell asleep on the swing."

"Who are you?" the woman asked. "Are you her husband? Well, you'd better keep her on a tighter rein, mister. Any woman who'd wander around at night deserves just what she got, especially one out wandering around when it's raining. She must've enticed my husband for him to pick her up and carry her upstairs. She did have her arms around his neck right tight when I opened the door. Must've changed her mind about her mission when I opened the door. Well, she'd best not go to the authorities, because I saw what I saw and I'll sure tell it. Woman like that don't deserve to be married. Come on, Alvin. Maybe you've learned a lesson that'll keep you from drinking from now on."

Alvin shook his head from side to side, trying to make sense of the whole ordeal, and followed his wife into their room. She slammed the door and the noise that filtered through let everyone know the fight was not over.

"I'm not . . . I didn't . . ." Adelida looked up into Rueben's eyes. Doors began to softly close down the hallway.

He opened the door to his room and motioned her inside. She folded her arms across her chest and sat down in an oversized, oak rocking chair. "I couldn't sleep. The window had to be closed because of the rain and it was so muggy. I just went down to the porch for a breath of fresh air and sat down on the swing. I didn't mean to fall asleep."

Rueben rubbed his eyes.

"Aren't you going to say anything?" she asked.

"I'm not your husband. I'm not anything to you, Adelida. If you'd wanted to take that man to your room, it would have been your business."

"I didn't," she protested. He'd just said she was nothing to him. Or had he? How had he said that anyway?

"I suppose if we're to have any sleep, we'd best share

this room," he raised the window an inch or so, letting the warm, night breeze flow into the room. "That should keep you alive. You take the bed and I'll finish the night on the floor."

"I don't think so, Yankee," she seethed. "The floor is mine. Right below that window where I can breathe in the fresh air. Besides, I wouldn't dream of taking your bed, not when you should have jumped right out there and demanded to know what that man was doing carrying your wife up the stairs."

"My wife?" Rueben's temper flared.

"Yes, your wife. I'm wearing your ring. We're registered as Mr. and Mrs. Rueben Hamilton even if we do have two rooms. Remember? His wife is sure enough mad at him even if she did defend him when she thought you'd go to the sheriff when daylight comes." Adelida ripped a quilt from the bed, snatched one of the two feather pillows and curled up on the floor, turning her back to Rueben.

"Don't you talk to me like that," he said. "Why should I jump on some silly, drunk man who made an honest mistake? Even in the light of the hallway I could see that you two looked alike. Same colored nightrails, same hair. It was just an error in judgment. Why did you let him carry you, anyway?"

"Because I thought he was you," she sat up and glared at him.

"Oh, sure you did. He's not one thing like me. He's shorter, heavier, rounder in the face, brown-eyed," Rueben shook his finger at her.

She was on her feet instantly, slapping his finger away. "And I'm supposed to see all that in the dark when I'm asleep? I was dreaming that you rode into a family picnic and swept me up on your horse to take me away so I wouldn't be killed in the war." She wished instantly she could take the words back. She meant nothing to him. He didn't even care if she turned into a lady of the night.

"Likely story," he said, biting his lower lip to keep a grin at bay. "Let's go to sleep now. It's still a long way to Love's Valley. That is, if you've a mind to go see the mountains. Maybe you'd rather stay in Baltimore?" So she dreamed of him rescuing her. That had to mean she thought of him as a knight in shining armor, the one who rode up on the white horse in the fairy tales and rescued the princess. Maybe she harbored some feelings for him.

"Men! This is enough." She turned away from him only to stumble over one of his shoes beside the bed and fall right into his arms.

His heart raced as fast and furious as her own. He crooked a finger under her chin, tilting it back so he could see her face by the moonlight. Such a beautiful woman. He bent and she tiptoed. Passion danced around the room like gypsy fairies at an Irish wedding. When his lips touched hers, she thought she'd died and gone to heaven. When he ran his tongue across her lower lip, her heart melted.

"Good night, Adelida," he whispered huskily when the kiss ended.

"Bonsoir," she whispered just as hoarsely.

I love you, he thought as he laid his head on the pillow.

Je t'aime, she thought.

Chapter Fifteen

Adelida ate scrambled eggs and hot biscuits in the hotel dining room and read a newspaper at the same time, keeping both her mind and eyes off Rueben, who read his own paper. The young couple from the night before occupied a table not ten feet from Adelida and Rueben. They were together, but it was very evident that they hadn't settled their differences yet.

Adelida eyed them carefully. It was a complete mystery how she'd ever mistaken that short, chubby fellow for Rueben, even in her sleep. Rueben, who didn't have a spare ounce of fat on his muscular body, who was six feet tall and had arms like a dock worker. The other man's baby face was as round as a cantaloupe. His beady little eyes and puffy mouth didn't look one bit like Rueben. If she'd been fully awake she would have realized from the beginning that he wasn't the love of her life rescuing her from a horrible war.

Rueben noticed the couple when they came into the room. He felt foolish for ever saying that the woman looked enough like Adelida to warrant the drunk man's mistake.

The woman sitting across the table from the man was short-er and much heavier than Adelida. Her hair was light brown where Adelida's was as black as a moonless midnight. Her lackluster eyes were some non-descript shade of green. Adelida's were a dark brown. And the woman had a pinched little mouth that didn't beg for kisses like Adelida's did.

The kiss last night had left him with a jumble of mixed emotions. At least it would all be over in just three more days. Surely by the time they reached Love's Valley, there would be a letter from Reed with a report as to how much money should be paid to Adelida.

They boarded the train at Mount Clare Station at noon, and by one o'clock Adelida had leaned her head on his shoulder and slept soundly until five o'clock that after-noon when they reached Martinsburg, Virginia. Following supper in the hotel, they went to the room Rueben had rented. It was a nice, big room with two double beds, cov-ered in snowy white, ironed sheets. She sat in front of the open window, a shawl around her shoulders, and stared out at the people coming and going on the streets. Was that couple in love? The woman had her arm looped in his and they didn't seem to be in a hurry, just strolling along enjoying each other's company. She imagined a nice leisure walk with Rueben beside her like that.

"Penny for your thoughts," he said, watching her yearn-ing eyes. No doubt, she was wishing she was already back in her swamp.

"You ain't got enough pennies to buy my thoughts," she said, without looking at him. One look into those green eyes and she'd be falling into his arms again.

"You still planning on going back to the bayou once you've seen the mountains?" he asked.

"Where else would I go?"

They both fell silent. Each was tied up in their own aching hearts until bedtime. She crawled between the sheets, glad that she had her own bed, even if Rueben was right across the room in the other bed, and that the window could be opened so she could have fresh air. She used the pillow to catch the tears she cried when she thought about telling him good-bye for the final time.

The stagecoach was worse than the one she had ridden from Houma to New Orleans. If there was a pothole, the driver managed to hit it twice. Dust boiled up from the tires and settled on everything in the coach—on her face, her skirt, her bonnet, Rueben's hat, his shoes. By the time they reached the station in Mercersburg, Pennsylvania, they both looked as if they'd rolled in it. Supper had already been served at the hotel and the dining room closed for the night, but the clerk managed to find them a loaf of bread baked just that day, two slices of fried ham, and a chunk of cheese.

"So tomorrow we arrive in Shirleysburg. I feel like a little boy on Christmas morning," he said. "It's been fourteen months since I was home, and then only for a couple of weeks. Before that it was four years. I may not leave the valley for a year. My sister was just a little girl and now she's engaged. My brother is married and expecting a baby this summer. My cousin, who is like a sister to me, is married. So many changes to get used to."

"Family," she cut a slice of cheese with her jewel-bedecked knife. "Must be nice to have family."

They finished their supper in silence, again each in their own realm of thought, each dreading the final day when the journey would end. Neither opened their hearts to express what was hidden there. Tiredness brought fitful, dream-filled sleep.

The mountains were there when she awoke the next morning, off in the distance, beckoning for her to come and see. In spite of the dust and a rough road, she kept her head out the window gazing at the scenery. Rueben had trouble keeping still himself and enjoyed watching her excitement. When they reached Fort Loudon and really got into the mountains, she all but squealed.

"It's just as I thought it would be," she said. "It smells like I imagined. Look at those ferns, Rueben. Did you see that deer? It jumped right up the side of that mountain. Oh, it's beautiful. Does your valley look like this?"

"Yes, I saw the deer. No, my valley doesn't look like this. This is the side of a mountain. If you look out my side you'll see the drop-off and the valley down below," he said, seeing things through her eyes.

In the middle of the afternoon, the stage stopped at Shade Gap. Adelida bounded out, dusted off her skirt and followed Rueben inside the weathered wood building.

"Bad news," the coach driver said, coming in right behind them. "Got a wheel that isn't going another mile. Got room for these two for the night? Me and the shotgun rider can sleep out in the stable with the horses. We might get the wheel fixed 'fore nightfall, but won't be getting any more miles in today."

"What?" Rueben turned so quick that he ran into Adelida and had to steady her by wrapping his arms around her.

"You heard me, Mr. Hamilton. Got us a wheel that's about to fall off. I'll have to do some blacksmithing to get it repaired by bedtime," he said.

"This is not a hotel," the stationkeeper said. "You're welcome to the hay loft, but that's the best I can do."

"You got a horse and buggy you'd be willing to rent us?" Rueben asked.

"Sure. I could do that, but how'd I get it back?" The man shook his head. "Where you going anyway?"

"Do you do business with anyone in Shirleysburg?" Rueben asked. "I'm headed for Love's Valley, but I'd return it to Shirleysburg tomorrow afternoon."

"That'd be just fine. Livery man over there is kin to my wife. They'd be glad for an excuse to bring the rig home," he said.

"Then we'll be obliged if you'd get it ready and we'll be on our way," Rueben said.

"Going to Love's Valley? You a Hamilton?"

"Yes, I am. Rueben, the middle son."

"Knew your Pa right well. Good man. Your Ma's done well since he died. Keeping it all together. You the one that went off to Georgia?" The man eyed Adelida, not missing the ring on her finger. "Your Ma know you're bringing' home a rebel woman?"

"No, thought I'd surprise her," Rueben chuckled. "I'm the one that the President sent to Louisiana. This is Adelida, my wife."

"I'm right glad to make your acquaintance, sir," she said.

"I'm glad your Pa isn't alive to see what's come of his bloodlines."

"I hope you aren't insulting my wife," Rueben said tersely. "Just to make sure you understand something, my father would be honored to have Adelida in our family. He wouldn't appreciate anyone slurring any woman his sons decided to bring into the family."

"No insult intended," the man said, setting his jaw tightly. "I'll get that rig ready now. You two get your belongings off that coach out there and you can get on your way. Be dark now before you get home."

Rueben had a difficult decision to make when he reached Orbisonia. He could take the shorter route to Love's Valley and show the whole valley to Adelida—that would involve getting home at dusk and she'd have to spend the night with the family—or he could drive another four miles to Shirleysburg, get Adelida a room in the hotel there, and go home alone. He slowed down at the outer edge of town, unable to make the decision.

"So, is this Shirleysburg?" she asked.

"No, this is Orbisonia," he told her. "We can have a bite of supper here at the hotel. Afterwards, I thought maybe we'd go through the valley so you could see all of it. If you'd be willing to stay at my house tonight, that is. But if you'd be more comfortable in the Shirleysburg hotel, I'll take you there."

"No, no. I'll sleep in the back of the wagon if they don't want me, Rueben. I want to see the valley. I want to see if the house there is like the one in the picture I saw when I was a little girl," she said. It was an answer to a prayer. Just one more night in the same house with him.

"I don't think you'll have to sleep in the wagon," he laughed. "Even if Ellie and Colum are still in the main house there's still rooms to spare, plus there's a bunk house."

"Oh," she said, her pretty mouth making a perfect little O.

The sun, barely a sliver over the mountaintop, hung there as if waiting for them. The house loomed—big, sturdy, and ominous in the setting sunlight. It was a red brick with two white pillars gleaming by the dim light against all that dark brick.

"It's beautiful," she whispered in awe. "I've really seen the mountains and the house, and it's just like the picture."

Before he had time to answer, the front door opened and a woman shaded her eyes with the back of her hand against the last rays of daylight. She leaned back into the house and yelled, "Here comes Henry Rueben," and then bounded off the porch to meet them as soon as the buggy came to a standstill.

Rueben left Adelida sitting on the springy seat. His mother, a lovely middle-aged woman with a smile on her face, hugged him. His brother clapped a hand on his shoulder and shook his hand, a big grin covering his face, so much like Rueben yet not nearly so handsome by Adelida's standards. A young lady ran out of the house, jumped from the porch into his arms and planted kisses all over his face. Another stood back, waited her turn, and then hugged him.

"Rueben, I want you to meet my husband, Colum Sullivan," she took the man who'd been standing back just inside the house by the hand and brought him forward. "We were married last month."

"And this is Douglass," Monroe motioned for his very pregnant wife to join him.

"And who is this?" Indigo let go of him long enough to stare rudely at Adelida.

"It's Rueben's surprise," his mother laughed. "Harry Reed wrote me a letter. Just came today and said Rueben was bringing a big surprise, but I wasn't to tell any of you. So let me do the honors, son. Everyone, this is Adelida. I do hope I said your name right. She's from the bayou country of Louisiana and she's Rueben's new wife."

"You brought home a rebel woman?" Indigo's eyes widened. "Not you, too, Rueben. You're the one who had some sense. The dull brother who wouldn't do such a thing. Lord, I don't think I can stand it."

"Don't you call him dull, and sugar, you can stand it," Adelida said.

"Well, pardon me all to pieces," Indigo flared up at her new sister-in-law. "He's my brother and I'll call him what I want."

"Guess I'd better explain something," Rueben had it on the tip of his tongue to tell them Adelida wasn't his wife.

"You should've thought of that before you up and married a woman like her," Indigo said.

"Indigo, I think that's enough," Monroe said. "You're bordering on slurring both Douglass and Colum with your smart mouth."

"I'll slur whoever I want. Am I the only one in this family who's got a lick of sense? You'd think the war would have taught you all not to trust those kind of people," Indigo shouted at Monroe.

"The war took all three of my brothers from me," Adelida hopped down, swept her skirts to one side, and bowed up to Indigo. "If there's any mistrust to be handed out, lady, it would be me not trusting the likes of you. Now Rueben has driven hard and long to get here before the day's end and you are spoiling his homecoming. I do believe a sister who truly loved her brother as much as I loved mine would apologize and watch her sharp tongue."

"I will not," Indigo huffed. "I already don't like you. Rueben deserves better than a Southern woman the likes of you."

"Well, *cher*, he deserves better for a sister than you, too. But I guess he's pretty well stuck with the both of us right now. As we say in the Acadia, *c'est ein affaire a pus finir*. It means 'it's a thing that has no end.' We can stand out here and argue all night but to no avail. Shall we go inside the house and let the rest of your family make your brother welcome?"

Laura Hamilton, the mother, giggled and Douglass joined her. Indigo had met her match one more time. "I'm thinking," Laura said, "that Adelida is right. Let's not stand out here arguing. Let's go inside and get to know the newest Mrs. Hamilton."

Chapter Sixteen

Adelida had intended to own up that she wasn't the newest Mrs. Hamilton as soon as they were in the house. But Indigo's attitude changed her mind. That, and the fact that Rueben was sitting right beside her, his thigh pressed against her leg on the settee in the parlor while everyone seemed to talk at once. For just a little while, she told herself, just for an hour, she'd be a part of a big family again, one which lived in a house on dry land just like in the book. She'd pretend she was really the newest Mrs. Hamilton and the handsome Rueben was her husband.

"I'm more than a little tickled to have another Southern woman in the family," Douglass whispered, lowering herself into an overstuffed chair beside Adelida. "Don't mind Indigo. She's all bark and no bite. Full of spit and vinegar, but under it all, she'll come through for you. She'll fuss and fume, but if anyone else says a word about you being unworthy of the almighty Hamilton name, she'll fight them tooth, nail, hair and eyeballs unto the bitter end. It's just the way she is. Tomorrow you'll have to come visit mine and Monroe's home. It's just up the valley a little ways. Colum and Ellie have begun to build one too. I expect you and Rueben will be thinkin' along those lines before long."

"I suppose," Adelida muttered. Tomorrow she'd be long gone and there would never be a house in this lovely valley for her.

"Did you two have your supper?" Laura asked. "Forgive my bad manners, but I was so excited to look up the lane and see you coming home, I forgot to ask about food."

"We ate in Orbisonia," Rueben said.

They kept talking, everyone at once, without a quiet moment until Laura lit the lamps. Adelida stifled a yawn, hoping no one saw and thought they should end the day. She could easily sit there until morning, just listening to them laugh and visit.

"It's been a long day," Laura finally said. "Time for us to let these folks go to bed."

"We are pretty tired. We didn't even put the horse and buggy away. Colum and Monroe, could I get you to help drag that trunk out there upstairs? Adelida's got a set of silver in it that weighs a ton. But she wouldn't leave the island without it. Not even when the rescue ship came," Rueben said.

"Rescue ship?" Indigo asked.

"Didn't Reed tell you?" Adelida asked. "The first ship we started out on ran into foul weather. A full-fledged hurricane. Rueben and I almost drowned. Rain coming down so hard, we couldn't even see each other. Waves so tall they carried us halfway to heaven itself. We were slung onto an island with nothing more than what we were wearing. A big armoire washed ashore that had the silver in it, and I was determined to bring it with me."

"And that is a story to be told over breakfast," Rueben

said. "Right after which we will have to return that buggy out there."

"Don't think of it," Colum said. "I'll help Monroe bring in the trunk and then take care of the horses for you. You two go on up and get some rest. It's been a long trip. We'll help you get the buggy taken back tomorrow. We've got lots of time to hear all the stories."

"Be sure you make Rueben tell you about the spy and the treasure and not to forget the pink hotel in Charleston," Adelida said as Laura led the way up the stairs to the room she'd already prepared for Rueben and his new wife.

Laura lit a lamp in the corner of the room and opened the door out onto the balcony. "I know this is a big change for you. Reed said you were raised up on a houseboat in the swamplands. Please don't be offended by Indigo. She's been spoiled. The last child after three sons. Her father, and I'm afraid I'm guilty too, doted on her. We let her speak her mind freely, and she's not learned yet when not to do so."

"No offense," Adelida was drawn toward the balcony with the nightview of the huge mountain behind it. "And please don't feel bad toward Rueben when he tells you the whole story tomorrow. Sometimes when one takes a chance, they have to live with the consequences."

"Always," Laura said. "Now have a good rest, and we'll get to know each other better in the coming days."

Sure we will, Adelida smiled. *By the week's end, I'll just be a family joke.*

"Where do you want this, ma'am?" Colum asked, lugging the trunk into the door.

"Right there is fine," she smiled at him.

"You're right, it does weigh a ton," Monroe said. "Thank

goodness it won't have to be moved out again any time soon. You thinking about building a house in the Valley?" he threw over his shoulder at his younger brother.

"Might," Rueben said. "Right now I'm thinking about a good night's sleep with cool mountain air blowing through those doors."

"And a pretty woman to keep you warm," Monroe whispered so low only Rueben heard it.

As soon as the door was shut, Adelida's temper opened. "Why didn't you tell them? Now they'll think I slept with you tonight!"

"Because Indigo was being a brat. I can't believe she's old enough to be engaged and acting like that. It'll do her good to think I did bring home a Southern bride for a night," he sat down on the edge of the bed and pulled off his boots.

"And what are we going to do about the sleeping arrangements right here under your mother's roof, Rueben?"

"Didn't bother you to sleep on the floor of the hotel, did it? Matter of fact, if I remember right, you insisted on it. You want me to go out to the bunkhouse and give Indigo the satisfaction of knowing we're fighting? Or you want me to take the floor? I don't mind doin' either one."

She threw her hands up in despair. What she wanted was the right to fall backwards into that bed with him. She went out onto the balcony and sat down in the wide rocking chair over in one corner. She'd best find a comfortable position, because this was where she would be sleeping tonight.

Rueben joined her on the balcony. His tongue was glued to the roof of his mouth. She'd stood up to his sister, not because she was offended, but because Indigo had slighted him. She'd fit right into his family, rebel-rousing Southern woman that she was and all. And he loved her.

"Adelida," he shoved his hands into his pockets and turned his back to her. He'd been born a Northern man. He'd fought in the war on the side of the Union, had been on the side that claimed all of her brothers. They were as different as a sunlit day and the darkest, moonless night. He couldn't change what or who he was.

"Yes, Rueben," she said.

"I don't know how to say this. I never was good at words or courting women either. Not like Reed and Monroe. They always had a flock of pretty girls around them, but I'm just so plain spoken, I tend to run them all away."

"Spit it out," she joined him at the rail, close enough that he had to fight the urge to take her into his arms.

"I've figured out the heart and soul don't care which side a man fought or which side a woman was on either. It just sees what would make it complete and whole and that's why I'm trying to say—I'm afraid I'm making a blundering mess of it, but I've fallen in love with you," he said. "I didn't mean to. I fought it but my heart don't seem to give a damn if you are rebel or not. So there. Now what are we going to do about it?"

She had to grab the railing to keep from falling flat on her face.

"Don't laugh at me," he pleaded. "Just tell me that you're going to tolerate the night with me and go home to the bayou. But please don't laugh. You can have the bed. I couldn't sleep a wink anyway. I had to speak my mind."

"Laugh at you," she melted into his chest, wrapping her arms around his neck. "Laugh at you! Sugar, I love you so much my heart aches from it. Now you tell me what we're going to do about it."

A wide grin split his handsome face as he finally

looked down into her beautiful eyes and even prettier face. "I suppose we could go to the church, tell the priest our predicament and get married tomorrow. No one would ever have to know we didn't get married a month ago."

"Is that a proposal?" She laid her face against his chest and listened to the rapid beating of his heart.

"It is at that," he whispered.

"Then the answer is yes, Rueben. I will marry you tomorrow, but darlin' this is going to be the longest night we'll ever spend. I don't expect either of us will get much sleep, will we?"

"Don't suppose we will," he sat down in the rocking chair and drew her into his lap. "Why don't we just pass the night cuddled up together in this chair. Tomorrow we'll say our vows."

"Sounds like a good plan to me. You going to tell them about the amnesia?" She settled into his arms, fitting there perfectly.

"Some things a couple keeps secret, just between them, don't you think?" He kissed her eyelids, her nose and finally her mouth. "Do you think you can be happy here? It's not the bayou."

"Wherever you are, that's where I'll be happy. I love you, Rueben. And now could you kiss me one more time?"

"And I love you, Adelida. And yes, I'll kiss you one more time. And one more after that, and one more after that, forever."